2015

Writing from Inlandia

An Inlandia Institute Publication

Editorial Board

ISBN 978-0-9839575-9-1

Welcome to Writing from Inlandia!

This book contains windows into the hearts and minds of Inlandia's writers - writers who have spent the last year working closely together to produce the poems, essays, and stories that you see here. This is the fourth anthology in a series that we expect to continue for years to come.

Writing from Inlandia is an anthology of work by writers participating in Inlandia's Creative Writing Workshops program. This year's anthology contains work from five different locations: Corona, led by Matt Nadelson; Idyllwild, led by Jean Waggoner & Myra Dutton; Ontario, led by Charlotte Davidson; Palm Springs, led by Alaina Bixon; and Riverside, led by Jo Scott-Coe; a new sixth location, San Bernardino, led by Andrea Fingerson, has been working hard and will be eligible to submit work for the 2016 anthology.

The Creative Writing Workshops began in Riverside the summer months of 2008 with a single workshop in at the Riverside public library, led by Ruth Nolan. Over these past seven years, the workshops program has grown wildly. We are proud to call each of these writers Inlandians, and revel in their success.

Appreciation

This anthology would not exist without the talented and dedicated writers and workshop leaders who participate in Inlandia's Creative Writing Workshops Program, a sampling of whom appear here. It is only because of their hard work, and the time and dedication of Inlandia's Publications Committee members and volunteers, that this anthology was compiled, formatted, proofread, proofread again, submitted for review by the writers themselves, corrected, reviewed again, and then finally submitted for publication. Without that time and dedication we would have nothing to show for a year of good, productive writing—except, of course, the writing, which, thanks to all of them, you can now read here.

Inlandia's Creative Writing Workshops Program, related events, and annual publication of the Writing from Inlandia anthology are made possible by grants from the E. Rhodes and Leona B. Carpenter Foundation, the City of Riverside, and Poets & Writers Readings/Workshops Program, with particular thanks to the director of their west coast office, Jamie FitzGerald Lahey, and the James Irvine Foundation, funder of Poets & Writers Readings/Workshops Program. We also wish to thank Inlandia's members and the readers who make this anthology worthwhile. All of these sources contribute to the production of this anthology.

We also wish to thank our host venues for allowing us to use their space to hold our workshops: the Smoke Tree Racquet Club club house in Palm Springs, the Riverside Public Library downtown, the Corona Public Library, the Idyllwild Public Library, the Feldheym Library in San Bernardino, and the Ovitt Family Community Library in Ontario.

Inlandia is grateful for all of your support.

—Cati Porter, Executive Director

Contents

2015

Writing from Inlandia

Conflicting Visions

This desert will be the death of you. Dry lands choked with sandy soot. All of California's dirty exhalations settle here in this forgotten valley that once yielded lush fields of orange and grapefruit orchards.

You came from the Emerald City on the Pacific. You felt the wet kisses of the Puget Sound on your brow at Pike Street Market. You discovered fresh fish at Ivars. You supplied your childhood tea sets with all of the herbal tea varieties the original Starbucks had to offer.

Now you haunt random Starbucks chains no longer sipping tea but slurping espresso by the double shot. Trying to stay awake during your haze filled stifling hot days. Consume bits of Yellowtail, Salmon and Albacore at all-u-can-eat sushi buffets to sustain the taste of brine on your tongue.

He has invited you to come live with him in his city by the sea. But you stand hovering in indecision.

Celena Diana Bumpus

Some Ideas Skim The Surface

Floating bubbles carried on the gentle breath of June.
Thin skins threatening to tear with every gust of wind.
Shimmering iridescent, they capture an audience.

Celena Diana Bumpus

Succubus Loved

I will bathe in your obsessive kisses
oil my skin in your helpless tears
pop bath bubbles of your breathless chuckle
burn a candle to hold my moods at bay
wash away the cloying scent of my past lovers

Goat Curry

The cold water in the sink flowed heedlessly over the metal colander making a faint cymbal crash as it cascaded over sugar snap peas, navel orange colored peppers and eggplant the color of fresh bruises.

She stood next to the sink, chef's knife gripped in hand methodically julienning carrot slices. Her caramel colored hands with magenta colored knuckles swiftly cutting in wet rhythm. The pot on the stove frothed with steam. The water is a turbulent sea of curry, turmeric, goat meat, garam masala and parsley.

Brushing the carrot slices into the bubbling water, she reached blindly into the sink. Her hand following the contours of the colander to grab a round vegetable inside. Drawing one out she was faintly surprised to see the royal purple aubergine in place of a sunset colored pepper.

With a sigh, she pulled her cotton turquoise sleeve down over her own purple echo and decisively chopped the eggplant in half.

2:03 a.m.

Sleep becomes a rabbit fleeing from a fox. The fox now borrows
every memory from everywhere in the glade. I hide in the tall grass, cloves,
and lavender hoping to catch sight of the rabbit or fox. I laid sharp
snares at acute angles.

Darvon are dogs on the heels of the hare. The fox keeps
distracting the hounds from their hunt, hoping to steal their prey away.

The rabbit abandons its warren for a bramble patch.
At one end the fox yips. At the other, the hounds howl like mad.
I arrive, but again I'm too late to rescue the rabbit.

Random Thoughts

While riding the Metrolink from Riverside, CA to Buena Park, CA

I.

Woman seated perpendicular to me highlights passages
in her bible with an ink pen. I look out at the same landscape
I pass every Friday evening on my way to Buena Park. I feel
crappy for making a Bitstrip mocking her and my other car mate
for being stinky in forty-three percent humidity. I am lucky
to be breathing — 2 inhalers, one antibiotic, one steroid prescription,
and 4 allergy pill bottles and I should have nothing to say.

The woman does not speak English but has the biggest, brightest smile
at the end of such a stressful day. I envy her energy and her shiny
view of this ordinary commute. *King and Lionheart* by Of Monsters
and Men, is playing on my Samsung.

II.

Drawing closer to Orange County and my Golden Eagle, tension
tightens its grip on my shoulders. I am afraid of missing him. Afraid
of feeling captured. He calls me his wildcat. At times I feel collared,
We've been together for 6 months. I don't know if I am relieved
or scared. Are we sinking or swimming? Am I?
I fear the idea of forever with him. I fear another 6 months.

I wish I could follow this lady traveling on the train. Get off where
she gets off. Just disappear for a little while. Run away silently
with someone who does not understand my language
so when I cry I don't have to explain why.

III.

Wedged in this corner seat with my rolling case filled with
student manuscripts, loose unpublished poetry of my own
and clothes I will never wear this weekend. I am slowly moving
more of myself into my Eagle's nest. Each week promising myself
I will drive to his city near the sea and remove all trace of me
from his home. Instead, I find another excuse to leave
my car with my mother.

IV.

13 minutes before detraining. Heaviness drags my final steps
into my Eagle's arms. Mustering a smile barely registering in my eyes.
I no longer recognize myself on these trips. This permeating sadness
I don't understand. The sun sets earlier these days and my sunglasses
hide much. Causing me to trip in the darkness. His hand holds mine
but his arm is never there to hold me when I stumble.

Celena Diana Bumpus

The Spotlight, Harsh

I am always shivering in my loosely
draped dresses, because you like my
feminine side.

I am standing inside a glass enclosed metal
box on an empty stage, you are my only
audience.

You watch my every facial flicker,
measuring my love and devotion--every thought
that flits wordlessly across my mercurial features.

I've learned to respond to your questions by naming
songs. You fail to decode the nuances in the lyrics.
Still you find me impossible to read.

You tell me everything should be in terms of black or white.
I tell you our very existence as a couple debunks
monochrome theories. I tell you you must learn to embrace
our various hues of pewter, gunmetal, dove, and silver.

Celena Diana Bumpus

Eastside, Riverside, Ca

Tight enclaves of low-income housing cluster on the Eastside of Riverside. Roughly, one and half miles below the University of California. I practice Spanish with curious immigrant neighbors and market store clerks. Some days I am too tired to remember the simplest of conjugations. Though I have known the head of the local gang and his family for several years, I have never bothered to ask the name of the gang. On my drives through the neighborhood to teach at the local senior center, gang names are inconsequential. I have lived in my sea green apartment since leaving my career with Child Protective Services and County Probation in 1999. My past is of no concern.

Instead, my neighbors and I share the present with *burria* tacos, shots of Patron, hair color advice, fighting techniques, court translations, *musica espanol*, carpools to dance clubs, fresh fruit and medical advice.

Lingering

My favorite French bakery in
Balboa Beach, CA made
the most wispy truffles of the finest Swiss chocolate.
You and I would visit nearly every weekend.

At Balboa, you proposed to me on the pier.
Your bittersweet words lingering like truffles
in my mouth as you kissed me.

One time we visited, the baker told us
he would no longer make chocolate
truffles and filled pastries.
The imported chocolate was too
expensive.

Between us, the bitter replaced the sweet.
I gave you back your engagement ring.
You returned to Melbourne.

Months later, I looked for our bakery.
I could still smell the Swiss chocolate
lingering at the door of the empty shop
when I peaked inside.

At Dusk

Dusk,
the day reluctant,
dallies
until
night's slinking darkness
slides
across the heavens
to snuff
its west'ring
glow.

Sylvia J. Clarke

Deadwood

When mood like soggy sand
      Weights the soul,
No "flights of fancy" soar
      Or words roll
In cadence from the pen.

Instead, ponderous ploddings
      Plunk to earth—
Dead wood, sodden,
      Of no worth
To ax or fire or fen.

Sylvia J. Clarke

Haiku for Mom

You, Mother, in pink
Petal rich flower blooming
Forever, I think.

Words

Silently some slip
through my muddled mind and slide
seamlessly away.

Sylvia J. Clarke

Where I Live . . .

Inland, its
     Nuanced
          Location
               Affords
                    Nearby (needed)
                         Domicile

Encircled by
     Mountains—a
          Protected,
               Invigorated,
                    Resourceful
                       Efflorescence.

GAP

"Here I'm wearing my best blue pencil skirt, and Grandma says, 'Don't you think that skirt is a bit too short? Modesty is important, you know.'" Ginger paced back and forth, her brows twisted in distress as she shared with Mother what had just happened. "This skirt is perfectly modest," she added, a foot stamp accenting the last two words.

Mother nodded her sympathy and agreement. "Remember, Ginger, Grandma comes from an entirely different era where women had to be sure to have at least three quarter length sleeves and wear skirts well below the knees. Try not to be too hard on her."

"I know, Mom," Ginger growled, rolling her eyes as she grabbed her backpack and headed out the door for school. Mother sighed.

A little later Mother stepped into the study/library. There she found Grandma, in tears and on her knees by a pile of books, searching for quotes on modesty.

Alteration

Red blood turns black when it drips into the dirt. Stacy learned that when she went looking for her dog Tippy and discovered him lying at the edge of the country road—dead. Seeing the mangled form of her beloved pet sent a chill down her spine and twisted her stomach. She turned and ran towards home shouting, "Mama, Mama! Tippy's been run over!" Blinded by tears, Stacy burst into the house and fell into Mother's comforting arms.

While she waited for Daddy to come home, images of Tippy's black coat matted with blood and dirt haunted Stacy. She wandered around the house in a fog of grief. Finally, Daddy came and retrieved poor Tippy's body, dug a hole, and helped Stacy bury him under the old pear tree outside the kitchen window.

That evening, as the family talked about their lost pet, Stacy smiled sadly, remembering Tippy as a tiny puppy; Mama had squeezed maggots out from his milk-soaked chin. About that same time they named him for the bit of white fur at the end of his tail. She had loved him from that moment on.

The next day, Stacy walked slowly down the road, thinking of all the times she and her doggie had walked there together—Tippy sniffing and exploring under the blackberry bushes along its edges—until she reached the spot where she had found him yesterday. She stopped. Nothing was left but the black stain of his blood in the dirt.

#

Wil Clarke

Sonnet for Sylvia Nelson

It is but a season, Life but a stage,
We, but players, condemned by circumstance
To love, but give no expression; nor rage
Against the fate that has frozen romance,
Stopped the course of nature and our true Love.
Education, money, social pressure,
Impediments to our sanctioned above,
Together life. That a greater fissure
Has not appeared is truly a wonder
Than just one hundred miles away from you.
A year and more partitioned asunder,
We must exist although few others do.
God give us grace to endure this, our state,
That the season's end may remove the grate.

A Spoonerism

The *cozy little nook* in my cabin in the hills had sun shining into it every morning. I would take my private journal with me as early as the sun came in and write some stream of consciousness. When something would suggest itself, I would latch onto it and do exploratory writing about it. These could have to do with my concept of God and faith and grace. They could be something about how a merchant cheated me. They often had to do with the delightful fauna and flora in this mountain retreat. They could be something about "the help", especially the kitchen "help" I had employed.

She could be quite charming. If I happened to be in the mood, I might imagine, in my journal, a romantic little tryst with her. I could equally imagine her burning my toast or putting that detestable quinoa into my morning eggs or tea just to spite me.

After writing for an hour or two, I would put on my hat and shoes and take the dog out for a morning walk. We would race through the forest in imaginary pursuit of rabbits or coyotes. We often wandered along staring at the wildflowers to see if a new species had suddenly come to life.

When I returned to the cabin one day, "the help" was slamming pans together, throwing the glassware against the stone hearth, and spilling all the cereal onto the floor. She looked at me and yelled, "You lousy, dirty-minded old man!" and other unprintable slurs. She flung my journal violently at me. She had received strict instructions never to read my private journals. I had to let her go, the *nosy little cook*!

William the Conqueror

It was so close I could taste it. Edward the Confessor, King of England, was ailing. He was my father's first cousin and had no heirs. In fact it was rumored that his wife was frustrated with his inabilities. I had been Edward's favorite cousin. He had given me to understand that, when he passed on, I would inherit the kingdom.

That miserable little runt, Harold Godwinsson, was buttering up Edward to the point that it began to appear that the kingdom would pass on to him. Then just yesterday, February 14, 1066, a messenger from England arrived and told me that Edward had died and Harold had been crowned king.

Now, I'm not about to lose out on anything I really want. Take the case of Maud. She is a beauty to behold. I had been introduced to her during that magnificent joust near Lille. It was love at first sight. The skin of her face and bosom was white, smooth, and flawless. Her rich gown accentuated her figure. She couldn't take her eyes off of me either, and I sensed she more than appreciated my skill on the horse and my handsome, powerful physique. I decided then and there that she should be my bride, my queen.

Choosing some most imposing representatives, I sent them the three weeks' ride back to Flanders to ask for her hand in marriage. She was insulted. She was furious. She responded instantly that she was much too high born to stoop to marry the bastard son of a tanner's daughter. She was referring to the fact that my father, Duke Robert, had consorted with the young and alluring commoner, Herleva, and I was the happy result. This was before she settled down and married Herluin de Conteville. Since I'm the duke's only son, he watched over me with keen fatherly interest and trained me to be the fearless warrior I am today.

At the time when I sent my delegation to Flanders to win Maud's hand, I was struggling with several mighty nobles who each wanted to rule Normandy. There was no way I could let Maud's unfortunate words ruin not only my love for her but also my tenuous hold on Normandy.

My trusted bodyguard, my half-brother Odo, and I mounted our fastest steeds and in six hard days covered the 250 miles to Lille. It was Sunday, and Maud, dressed in all her finery, was just coming from church when I rode up.

Racing my horse up next to hers, I grabbed her by her long braids and threw her into the mud. Springing from my horse, I landed next to her. I berated her mercilessly for insulting me, my background, my heritage, and my dear mother. I made a big show of beating her. It was purely for show and scared her but little. In one swift leap, I jumped back onto my horse, turned around, and raced back towards home before her father could take any action.

Count Baldwin, her father, started to raise an army to punish my audacity. But Maud recognized that I was her best suitor and told her father in no uncertain terms that I was the only man she would marry. After a year or two I had patched up my relations with Baldwin, and we had a splendid wedding. It took Maud and me nine years to appease the pope, since my enemies had informed him that Maud and I were cousins. In fact, he excommunicated both of us for consanguinity. We each had to build an abbey to appease him enough to get his special dispensation.

As I told you before, I'm not about to lose out on that kingdom. After all, a king is much nobler than a mere duke. And Maud, that beautiful duchess of mine, she may be short, but what she lacks in stature is easily overshadowed by her ambition to become queen. With her great wealth she has already bought me the great ship Mora to lead the Norman fleet as I invade England. I will be King of England.

Afterword:

I am descended through William and Maud's fourth son, the only son to be born in England: England's King Henry I.

Gateway Rock

Ryan, Jason, and I were climbing up Gateway Rock in Joshua Tree National Park. We had no climbing equipment except good Five-Ten approach shoes with rubber that grips granite tenaciously. The sun beat down mercilessly from the deep blue sky with no breeze to take the edge off the heat.

Near the top a giant boulder nestles against a cliff face. The face has two fissures in it. One is deep enough to wedge a climber's body into it, and by brute force and good shoe rubber, he can force his body upward. It is the route I have always taken. The other fissure has good handholds most of the way, but it is entirely exposed. I have never attempted that route more than half way up to help someone who was stuck on the cliff face. All three of us scaled the cliff and then returned to the boulder. The only safe way off this boulder is down the north side in a conveniently situated right-angle chimney.

Ryan had more training than either Jason or I. Besides he had taught a rock climbing course several times at La Sierra University. He decided to go down the south face of the boulder. I felt my stomach contract in fear. Two factors make this very difficult and dangerous. The granite on that side is loose and treacherous, and the face of the boulder curls under in a nasty negative slope with no handholds. There is at least a ten foot drop onto a steeply sloping rock below it.

My fear forced me to say, "I wouldn't even attempt that climb." Ryan is a big man, probably weighing as much as Jason and me combined. "But you are the rock-climbing teacher, so I'm not going to stop you" (as if I could have stopped him). I went on to describe my reasons for not attempting the climb.

Ryan was still anxious to give it a try. I reminded him that we had no ropes or other safety equipment. He started down cautiously.

Jason and I raced down the safe route to try and get below him so we could possibly spot his feet and break his fall. Before we were able to get down and run around the boulder, we heard him fall. A moment later we found him sitting on the steep slope of the base rock gripping his right ankle and moaning in pain.

The initially severe pain eventually ebbed out, and Ryan ventured to try and stand up. Instantly pain stabbed his ankle like a red hot knife. There was no way he could put any weight on it at all. I looked at Ryan, realizing he must weigh close to three hundred pounds. How could we ever get him down?

With the fierce sun turning us all into masses of dripping sweaty flesh, Jason and I got on either side of Ryan and held him up as we walked a few yards. He had an arm around each of our shoulders, and we supported his entire weight each time he moved his left foot. Shortly we came to the edge of the base rock he had fallen onto. We had to traverse sideways down an open space onto a somewhat lower rock. This move meant Ryan had to at least steady himself with his right foot and leg. Pain far worse than can be imagined shot through his whole body.

The parking lot was a long, long way down over a series of difficult traverses. For over an hour we inched our way from rock to rock. By the time we got to the parking lot, Ryan was absolutely exhausted from the herculean effort and the extended, extremely acute pain. Jason and I were also completely exhausted but at least not in pain.

We finally reached my car and got Ryan into the passenger seat. Jason climbed in back, and I drove Ryan down to his uncle's home in Palm Springs. On the way we stopped in Yucca Valley where Ryan had left his car. Jason drove it and followed us down the long pass.

Ryan's uncle took him to the hospital where an X-ray

showed he had broken his ankle. Ryan told me much later that he should have listened to me. I may not have his training and expertise, but I have a lot more experience scrambling on boulders than he does. When he confessed this, I resisted the urge to say "I told you so!"

Grace

What makes a motherless girl into a strong survivor? Her mother died when she was 5 leaving Grace, an older brother, George, and a baby brother, Elvin.

Her father didn't have a job and no one wanted to employ him because of his strong biphasic temperament. The neighbors stepped in and sent Grace and Elvin to the Cundells, a farming family who were unable to have children of their own. Grace had a long list of chores to be done before anything else each morning.

She decided to throw her whole being into getting these chores done and still leaving time to get to school. She had no time after school to do homework so she learned to do it during class. She found a friend in Jackie who would walk to school with her and help her organize what she had learned in school the previous day in such a way that she could remember it.

The Cundells needed someone to do all the chores in their dairy and when Grace turned 12 they told her that she must drop out of school and work full time on the farm. In winter time the howling, icy winds swept uninterrupted across the Kansas plains. There was no place in the barn where she could escape its icy fingers reaching into every part of her body. She worked on and Mr. Cundell noted that Grace was doing well at her work. She slaved away for over 5 years. She and a hired hand who was old enough to be her father planned to run away and get married as soon as she turned 18. Word got out about this to the local church she was attending and they raised enough money to send her away to a boarding school in another state.

She was a bright student and quickly pulled to the head of her class. She fell in love with Roscoe, a tall, sturdy farm boy from Michigan. He figured he would make a good farmer although he had higher aspirations. The two got married right after high school on October 22, 1939. Shortly afterward World War II started and Roscoe was drafted into the army and sent off to fight in France. Neither of them had any money and Grace worked at any job she could find to support herself and her new baby, Sylvia. It was not until 1945 that the couple were re-united.

(Written shortly after Grace's death at age 98.)

Deenaz P. Coachbuilder

*Iranshah Atash Behram-Eternal Flame

Symbol of the sun that nurtures all creation,
of energy love and happiness,
of the very spirit of Ahura Mazda,*
you were born from a merging of the hearths of sixteen fires.
From a blacksmith, the home of a learned *mobed*,*
a flame struck from lightning, you were consecrated
with the prayers of eminent Dastur Nairyosang and his wise priests,
in the city of Sanjan, two thousand and two hundred years ago.

Here you reigned, inspiring Zoroastrians who
traversed from afar to gaze with devotion at your unquenched fire,
for six unbroken centuries.
But fate would not allow you a somnolent sojourn.
Enemies of the faith invaded your peaceful city.
You were carried on tired and desperate shoulders
jostled through hilly forests inhabited by marauders
and unknown animals, moved to a secure place
in the mountains of Bharot, to protect you.

Nor would time shelter you there for long.
Your weary journey took you to five further destinations until
after many years you settled
on the sacred land of the city of Udvada.
Only the mighty and the pure of spirit
could have withstood a journey such as yours.

I travel a long distance for a glimpse of you, Iranshah,
from the tumultuous shores of America
to the quiet confines of ancient India's sleepy Udvada.

I walk along narrow dusty alleys and one storey houses.
A gaggle of gossiping teenagers,
the tinkle of bicycle chimes, an occasional car pass me by.

You live in a simple unassuming structure.
A silent *kushti* prayer and then, with bare feet
I step over the threshold of the chamber
of your house.
Hesitant, I tread forward, over the whispering steps
of a hundred pilgrims preceding me over time
across the deep maroon carpet that protects your sanctuary.

Quiet prayers sung by *miskin* mobeds*,
dedicated caretakers of the flame echo around me soothingly.
Through barred windows you beckon
gently uttering my name.
You draw me close, mesmerized,
climb through my pores and into my being.
Your flame scorches my hair and kindles my spirit.

I imagined you to be a robust, magnetic
all powerful force, sinewy arms leaping towards the ceiling
flames straining to burst that ornate silver *afargan*,*
flimsy walls confining a mighty burning force,
oh king of light and love and all living things.

Yet here you burn, no jeweled crown, no shrill bells,
no trumpets proclaiming your awesome unquenched longevity.
A soft warm glow, lemon magenta flames, a creamy gold

streaked with the orange of a million citrus trees,
outlined in heaven's turquoise sky,
rising from small knots of katha and sweet smelling sandal wood.

I place the ashes from your atash upon my forehead
and reluctantly prepare to leave.
Dare I turn my back? Will you be there when I return?

A honey gold aura reaches out and embraces me
its warmth melding in my veins.
Vibrations throbbing along nerve endings
whisper
"I will burn forever, till the ends of the earth."

My heart is filled with quietude
when I gaze into the mirror,
your sparks transform my pupils
into eternal flames.

---

* Iran Shah Atash Behram- a consecrated holy fire kindled and installed
in the 9th. century, a few years after Zoroastrians settled in the city of
Sanjan in India. The fire is called "Iran" in remembrance of the homeland
from which they fled, and "shah" for their famed Zoroastrian kings.
*Ahura Mazda- Lord wisdom, the sole divinity of the Zoroastrian faith,
the creator.
*mobed-Zoroastrian priest
*miskin-humble
*afargan-container

Deenaz P. Coachbuilder

Defenders

Dec. 11th. 2014

The "torture" report was released today...
Like many Americans, I abhorred
the images conjured-
  waterboarding
    enhanced interrogation
      death by hypothermia
terms ricochet like detritus
across our psyche.

Loneliness, pain, degradation
cloak these prisoners, caught
in the battles of 9-11.
Cruel and hardened terrorists as they are
theirs is the desperate awareness
of the abandoned.

An immigrant, I know that
the land I left behind
has been battered by atrocities
some recent, many buried
in the annals of history
Hindus, Muslims and Sikhs
in a mortal dance of spar and parry
as ahimsa fades further away.
Were they ever uncovered
each layer of the wound peeled
to expose the rotten core?
Some tried but were vilified.
The powerful remain.

Was I justified in placing my destiny
within the shores of this adopted land?
Is it still a dreamer's dream?

We have walked this way before
suspended civil liberties,
in the name of national security.
Does the beckoning ideal
yet glisten in the dark?

They were interrogators this time
who strove to acquire information
from those who hate us and would
suck away the very air we breathe,
to keep us safe and quiet and unbroken,
men of good faith gone awry, defending
our country, pawns on the chess board
of confused national politics.

We come to a bitter awareness
of our own ugly deeds, the breaking
of international norms created
to preserve warriors who find themselves
caught in the battles of a world
not of their making.

We deliberately expose our deeds.
  Self examination
  justification

acknowledgement
accountability
contrition.

Condemnation
rectification...

Deenaz P. Coachbuilder

the breath of a poem

I breathed in a poem last night

alphabets and exclamation points
multitudinous sentences
entire leather bound manuscripts
of verse
slid into my hungry brain

the faint blush of dawn
a butterfly's wing
an infant's first cry
melded magically into
my welcoming heart

I floated on currents to caress
the tops of the San Gabriel mountains
the knottiest existential queries dissolved
the root of Evil rotted away

pausing at the tip of an iridescent star
my "very flesh" became a poem

A companion piece to Mark Strand's "Eating Poetry."

Deenaz P. Coachbuilder

The Circle of Time

Time moved slowly,
the two year old
tripped forward
startled, balanced,
then learnt to sprint,
halting words
turned into torrents.

Time's passing
brought a mind filled
with knowledge,
the heart learnt
how to live
and love
and endure loss.
Curious spirit
knew no bounds.

Time's moments
stood in stark certainty
words etched unforgettably
each smile
each unshed tear
recalled with clarity.

Time leapt swiftly.
Limbs slowed.
One gray hair
multiplied

into a gleaming
halo
of white.

Time's memories warped
linear, circular
crisscrossed like meteors
fading untraced
into the night.

In the beginning
each door was obdurate
immovable, keyless,
puzzling, tantalizing.
Days struggled,
spirits retreated,
were enlightened,
retreated
unpredictably.

Time now stands still.
There is no waiting
just listening, living
seamless
the mysteries circle,
in a dance
that clings,
becomes
a state of love.

Silence surrounds,
and through it
the wind whistles
and sings,
a celebration
of every day things.

When they look into my eyes
I am a thousand
existential
miles away.

A lizard, descendant
of dinosaurs
performs his morning exercises
scrambling over rocks
that surround my door
and I
am at
the beginning
of
Time.

Deenaz P. Coachbuilder

The Jeweler

Lapiz and African rubies
Indian coral, rose amethyst
bejeweled butterfly broaches
gold bangles and rice pearl necklaces
sparkling stones of every hue,
he displayed his wares in my Mumbai home,
at the first ring of my telephone.

I offered him tea and biscuits,
at my instance, he sometimes took a mithai.*

One day, by chance,
I asked him about his wife.
His lustrous dark eyes welled.
My wife died last month.
After forty-five years, I am alone.

*an Indian sweet

Tigger

Tigger didn't fight when Carlos placed him in the cat carrier. Not a sound. None of his usual thrashing and biting. He was too tired from dragging his bloated belly, which sprawled over Carlos' left hand as he lifted Tigger into his traveling case.

* * *

The young veterinarian had learned to steel herself against showing or even feeling emotion, especially when she had to give bad news, but today it didn't work. These two silver-haired people were too anguished over their decision about their big handsome kitty with his incredibly soft, rich orange fur.

Swallowing and taking a deep breath, she forced herself to speak in modulated tones, which came out nearly matter-of-fact. She remained calm as she told them that there was no cure for Tigger's virus. The constricting membrane in his stomach would very soon begin crushing his vital organs and his current discomfort would quickly turn into severe pain.

"We can put his ashes in a little urn for you. Or we can have them strewn in the Pacific Ocean off Newport Beach. A service comes once a week to pick up all of our ashes."

The two responded with silence. Finally the man spoke. "Tigger always wanted to roam. We had him declawed when he was tiny, so we couldn't let him outside. But he spends hours going from window to window. He deserves his freedom. If there is a cat heaven, maybe he'll have fun with his new friends." He looked over at his wife to make sure he was on the right track.

"Do you want to spend a few minutes with him?" The veterinarian took them to a private waiting room with a long, green couch while she sent for someone to bring Tigger.

* * *

Tigger's heart leaped when he saw Grandma and Granddad. Lying on the couch between the two of them, nestled warmly against their thighs, he tried to forget the hour after hour of being probed, prodded, and pricked with needles. Hearing Grandma murmur "Hi, honey," Tigger managed a weak but grateful response.

As they gently stroked him, Tigger began to purr, softly but gratefully, a purr of rediscovered security. Free from those odd-smelling strangers who had been handling and poking him, he relaxed and closed his eyes. He was so relaxed that he didn't notice the veterinarian entering the room. Not until she took his paw did he open his eyes and see the vial full of liquid she was holding. "Not again," he thought. But at least now he was safe with Grandma and Granddad's loving hands caressing him. Feeling the calm that came with absolute trust, Tigger closed his eyes again and dozed off.

* * *

Laurel watched as the veterinarian slowly forced the liquid into Tigger's vein. She had prepared herself for that, but not for the moment when his purring abruptly stopped. A few seconds later, the vet placed the stethoscope against Tigger's chest, then nodded.

After the veterinarian left, assuring them that they could stay as long as they wished, Laurel continued petting Tigger. Her fingers brushed up against Carlos' hand, also stroking their adorable big fella, but she continued staring straight ahead at the wall.

* * *

Later, much later, they rose and left the room, saying nothing, incapable of looking back, afraid of looking at each other.

Carlos E. Cortés

Boy Scout Sash

My Boy Scout sash
  Eagle Scout pin
  Three palms
  Thirty-two colorful merit badges

Reptile Lore
  when I almost got bitten by a copperhead
Astronomy
  when we laid out on the parade grounds, told dirty jokes,
  and ogled Cassiopeia
Life Saving
  when we weren't grabbing each others'
  nuts under the water
Bird Study
  when we pretended we actually saw the little peckers
  during early morning nature hikes
Health
  when they scared the hell out of us with warnings about
  venereal disease.

Every badge has its story
and conjures up memories of the Boy Scouts
way back then
  when you never lied—or at least not too often—
    while holding up three fingers and saying "Scout's Honor"
  when you looked for old forty-something ladies
    to help across the street
  when you scraped snow and ice
    off your neighbors' driveways

when you snuck off and smoked in the camp latrine
when you learned to dance like Indians
   and make war whoops,
      never thinking it might be offensive
when "morally straight" in the Boy Scout Oath
   had nothing to do with sexual orientation.

Those were simpler times
or naïve times
or unconscious times
or protected times
that I often recall and wonder,
was it really that way?

Carlos E. Cortés

Hello. How Are You?

"Hello. How are you?"

I've read all kinds of stuff about
   human development
   generational changes
   getting older
   preparing for retirement
But none of that prepares you
   for the formidable challenge
   of answering that inevitable question
"How are you?"
   every day
   many times a day
   from all kinds of people
   close friends and strangers
   if there are such things as strangers
   in this brave new world
   where every clerk and phone voice
   insists on calling you by your first name.

So should I be honest
and spend the next ten minutes telling them
how I really am,
working my way from head to toe, explaining that
   my dandruff itches
   my right ear is ringing because of tinnitus,
     like it does every day, all day
   my back aches when I get out of bed
   the arthritis in my thumbs hurts like hell

my athlete's foot burns
I'm constipated as usual
but I had to get up at 4:30 a.m.
   to pee?

Come to think of it,
when people ask "How are you?"
they usually aren't trying to find out what time
I got up to pee,
so I guess I'll just keep it simple
and say fine.

Carlos E. Cortés

Self-Esteem

When I was growing up, nobody talked about self-esteem,
so I can't recall any people who helped build mine.
However, I do recall some of those
who didn't seem to give a damn about my self-esteem.
   The fourth grade teacher
      who threw erasers at us
      when we acted up.
   The boy scout counselor
      who told me I was too awkward
      to ever become a good Indian dancer.
   The high school coaches
      who seldom played me in football games that counted
      cut me from the basketball team
      never used me as a pinch hitter
      just because I was slow, puny, and uncoordinated.
   The factory supervisor
      who wouldn't let me drive a forklift
      even though I was nearly old enough.
   The high school girl
      who told me I couldn't touch her
      until we got married,
      even though I had never expressed
      the least interest in marrying her.
   The college German teacher
      who only gave me a B even though
      I came to class most of the time.
   The Army sergeant
      who woke up our barracks every morning by shouting
      "Drop your cocks and grab your socks."

The students
   who didn't give me perfect course evaluations.
The Dean
   who invited me to speak at her university
   but refused to pay me what I thought I was worth.
The literary agent
   who turned down my memoir
   by simply saying it was boring.

The list could go on and on,
but it does leave me wondering.
With so many people
who didn't give a damn about my self-esteem,
why do I wake up every morning
with a big smile on my face
when I look over at the grey-haired beauty
sleeping next to me?

Laurel V. Cortés

The Best-Fed Monarch

We know that Queen Elizabeth II-- as she enters her ninetieth year--eats a hearty breakfast of a cereal available to us all, sprinkled with fresh fruit from her gardens or some macadamia nuts that she keeps in a Tupperware box. She lunches on white fish with vegetables at 1 p.m. sharp. Four o'clock tea consists of scones, sandwiches and sugary treats. Dinner is at 8 p.m.: venison or salmon. The royal chef provides for 300 staff and visiting dignitaries, Presidents and such that may pop in from various countries around the globe.

But from all we have read, this diet may not qualify her as the best-fed monarch of all time. Who is, or was?

One candidate surely must be one of the Queen's predecessors, King Henry VIII. After all, upon his ascension to the throne in 1520 he did convert 55 rooms of downstairs Hampton Court Palace into a 3600 square foot kitchen so that 200-300 cooks could feed him and his 600-1200 courtiers. Henry and his gang ate spit-roasted wild boar twice a day (no refrigeration for leftovers). It showed off his wealth: few could afford to hire boys to turn the spit all day every day, and fewer still could afford the sugar, salt and peppers he provided for his entourage. His royal wranglings over spices with Venice, Lisbon and the Ottoman Empire are legendary. Who could match them?

Although pork was a daily staple, Henry did indulge in fish, peacocks (feathers reattached after roasting), wild turkey and other poultry, some lamb and beef. In his day raw vegetables were distrusted; veggies provided only 20% of the diet of the court. As for utensils, Caterina de' Medici brought two-pronged forks from Italy to France a few years earlier, but most English households carried only one or two. Henry might have had more, but 600? Why bother? What are two hands for?

White bread, ale, and sugared wine rounded out the menu, extended meal after meal, day in and day out. Desserts were not popular in England until the 18th century except for a spice cake on festival days, but Henry loved his strawberries in season. Historians cannot find another source of Vitamin C in the menu.

Ten pints of ale, 5,000 calories, and 20 grams of salt per day went into the royal body. Modern doctors agree that the Henry VIII had all the symptoms of Type II diabetes: failing eyesight, horrible leg ulcers, hypertension, and poor circulation. Henry was a giant (for his time) at 6ft 1 in. A recent analysis of his suits of armor reveals that his waistline grew from a svelte 32 inches in early manhood to an amazing 52 inches (over four feet wide?) before his agonizing death at the age of fifty-five.

We can look closer to home to find another candidate for best-fed monarch. Moctezuma II was killed in battle in 1520, (the same year that Henry VIII took the throne of England). His home was Tenochtitlán, built in 1325 on an island in Lake Texcoco, a muddy place between two volcanos inhabited now by Mexico City. Moctezuma's Aztec Empire stretched all the way to Nicaragua, and his city was one of the largest in the world, with 200,000 inhabitants. Every day the huge central market serviced 60,000 foodies who searched through the bounty before them for their evening fare.

Moctezuma was the ninth ruler of Tenochtitlán. He inherited an agricultural system of canals and dams--much like present-day Xochimilco--that engaged the ecosystem on its own terms. Out of this came 25 different fruits, including pineapples, lemons, limes, and pumpkins (remembering that tomatoes, maize, peppers, chiles, avocados, seeds, nuts [pecans, peanuts, and cashews], beans and squash are all technically fruits). Nopales, insects, vanilla, achiote, oregano, allspice, canella (a mild cinnamon), sweet potatoes, some forms of onion, fungi such as mushrooms, crayfish and other lake fish were available. Pulque, fermented from the juice of a cactus, was their specialty drink.

It was difficult for the average Aztec to hunt the wild turkeys and other poultry, wild boar, and rabbits, so their diet contained mostly fruits, fish and vegetables. They ground maize and flattened it into what we would call tortillas, providing a vessel for their food. Then as now, tamales, chiles verdes, pozole, and salsas with chipotles (an Aztec word meaning *smoked chiles*) were common fare.

Moctezuma himself ate spit-roasted meat (see what he and Henry had in common?), often wild turkey (much tastier than our bleached-out version), rabbit, duck, and dog--bred to be eaten. Because the royal family received tribute in cacao beans, the emperor drank hot chocolate (no sugar but with chiles and spices added, much like a present-day mole). Bees furnished honey, so the imperial diet did include nature's sweetener.

The Aztecs enjoyed a healthy and well-balanced diet; Moctezuma II should have lived longer than his 54 years (the circumstances of his death were described differently by every eyewitness!).

Alas, the Spaniards brought brand-new war technologies developed for their recent struggle to expel the Moors (1492): cannons and muskets, horses and, ah yes, small pox. (The fact that they also brought rice really did not matter at that point.) Sadly, the Europeans--with the help of disgruntled natives--systematically and totally destroyed the thriving 300-year-old Aztec culture in less than three years.

The term "best-fed" is open to interpretation. While for Henry best-fed was not well-fed, a nutritionist must applaud

Queen Elizabeth's manicured diet—the mellowed age of the royal couple should be taken as proof of its effectiveness. We may be sure that Sultans, Maharajas, Mandarins and Emperors have had pampered palates throughout the years.

But today, ordinary people's markets around the world can be amazing. Notably, those in Kenya abound with outstanding produce (including avocados as large as cantaloupes), world-famous coffee and Tusker beer. Also not to be missed: the unbelievable variety of spit-fired meats at Nairobi's incredible Carnivore Restaurant.

The topography of Kenya resembles that of California, so it is no coincidence that our own markets offer a similar variety (and freedom) of choice that incorporates all of the finest in produce, dairy, meat products, as well as exotic spices and recipes from around the globe. And unlike the Queen of England, we can eat any time we're hungry! I guess I'd just rather be me.

Laurel V. Cortés

Unrequited Love

Once on New Year's Eve, off the shore of Costa Rica
I danced on a ship in a gallant storm,
giddy with champagne and a tiny bit of fear
as we skidded back and forth across the floor
—along with tables, chairs, waiters and musicians

Once I tried to sleep in a vortex called Drake's Passage
below Cape Horn, where the
Pacific, Atlantic and Antarctic Oceans
collide in fury.
Pretty dreams come hard there.

Once I saw a diver down at La Jolla Cove
rise up spinning his legs above the water
with terror in his eyes.
His watch was found later in the belly of a shark.
That's a fact.

Once, when I was young, I watched a friend
ride the waves in Oceanside
when his surfboard, hard as the trunk of an oak
boomeranged off a wave into his chest
and killed him.

Lost fishing boats, overturned ferries,
sneaker waves, typhoons with tsunamis,
hurricanes with great names
—the epic debacle of Titanic—
lead us straight to this conclusion:

you can love the ocean
but she won't love you back!

Laurel V. Cortés

Private Thoughts in Haiku

The confines of rhyme:
Strife, so often paired with Wife
Or worse yet, with Life

***

Fourth of eight children:
Always someone to play with
Or to give you mumps.

***

The English language
Has no more deadly cliché
Than "Boys will be boys."

***

Okay, let's face it:
Hitler *liked* his hair that way
So does Donald Trump.

Noise

Have you ever stopped what you were doing to listen to the world around you? The quiet solitude that you might expect is not so quiet. Today's noise has polluted our surroundings —some pleasant, some irritating, some make you happy and then some make you angry.

Consider that Harley Davidson motorcycle driving by. Its rumble is a loud "vroom". To some it is obnoxious yet to others it is music to their ears. A social statement is make by the Harley cult. To feed this cult and protect that special and unique "vroom" Harley Davidson has patented the sound. Like it or not!

Sitting at home in the comfort of your favorite chair what is heard but the noise of the television with the sound filtering through the house. Being absorbed in your favorite program you are suddenly distracted by a passing siren of a fire truck, ambulance or police car. Some are passing all at once or at separate intervals. It's irritating.

Generally people love to make a statement with their cell phone ring. What a wide range of obnoxious, pleasant, funny and disturbing sounds that come from those phones. Of course, their is always some inconsiderate person in an audience who neglects to turn off that darn phone.

The latest car models are noise cocoons. The sound system complete with Sirius and multiple speakers. WiFi and Bluetooth so you can be connected to your world. You enter the car, reach for the ignition key - oh we're keyless now - start the car. The first thing you notice is the ding, ding of the seatbelt warning. If you put the transmission in reverse the backup camera comes to life and it sounds a warning if you come too close to an object behind you. Going forward their is an anti-collision sound if you get too close to the car in front of you. The famous "blind spot" signals a loud "deedle", "deedle" letting you know that someone is beside you. The once prevalent sound of the engine is now almost non-existent.

Walking down the street today you see people with wires coming out of their ears. They're entranced with phones blaring music or playing video games. Are they escaping the sounds of their surrounding, are they "dropping out," or is it just for stimulation? If you see an old person with wires in their ear, there is a good chance they are hearing aids.

The world has not gone completely mad with man made noises. There is hope. It is nice to escape to what might be considered the quiet of nature. Take a hike into the woods, the desert, or along a beach. Hearing the breeze rustle through the tree, the crashing of waves, or the stillness of the desert creates an inter-peace or a feeling of calm. To reach this calm and a time for personal reflection brave steps must be taken. The car must be parked, the cell phone muted and the i tunes shutoff. Now that that is accomplished start your hike into nature for that refreshing calm with the absence of invasive noises.

Holy Hassan

I was not in the driver's seat. I had been in Iran for ten months, and I still hadn't got behind the wheel of our car. One reason was that I didn't know how to use a stick shift.

Another was the fact that I had never bothered to get a driver's license, not even in California. While an undergraduate at UC Davis, I didn't need a car. Our tiny university town had more bikes than people. I thought nothing of pedaling back and forth to the art studios carrying a five-foot canvas that caught the wind like a sail. But even in that small universe, I lacked the confidence to drive. After I took out a neighbor's redwood fence during a driving lesson, I decided I was destined to be a passenger for the rest of my life. But my latest reason for not driving was the incomprehensible rat's nest that was Tehran's traffic.

I was terrified by the traffic, both as a passenger and as a pedestrian. The free-form crush was unfathomable to me. Lane divisions were mere suggestions. If a driver did not tailgate, another car would shape-shift itself into the tiny space in front of him. Taxis disgorged their passengers in the middle of the street. There were crosswalks, but pedestrians did not have right of way, so they crossed at their own peril. Even pedestrians with children in tow and laden with packages often ignored crosswalks altogether and dodged between passing cars with astounding impunity.

Rather than make things safer, Iranians left things up to God. Why bother with seatbelts or motorcycle helmets or traffic lights? They'd say, "I'll see you tomorrow, *ensha'allah*, God willing," just as they'd say, "I'll get my bachelor's degree in June, *agar khoda bekhad*, if God wants it." It was hubris to assume one could count on one's future plans, but was it also hubris to think one might affect that future by following a few basic safety rules?

If people are going to endure that kind of traffic, they need a worldview to deal with it. Before I moved to Iran, my husband's home country, I thought Kismet was just the name of some creaky 1950s Broadway musical. But I soon learned that the concept of kismet, or *ghesmat*, informs every aspect of Iranian life. The prevailing understanding was that what God wants is already set, that everyone has his or her *ghesmat*—an allotted portion or fate. Tehran traffic was the manifestation of that belief. That fatalistic worldview—comforting to so many believers—only served to make me feel more helpless—a passenger in a car I couldn't control.

Being a constant passenger freed up a lot of time for worrying. Ever since we arrived in Tehran, I had been making Ali nervous with my constant fearfulness--cringing, gripping the armrest, my back arched as I pressed my feet into the car's bulkhead, seeing potential catastrophe at every intersection. "OhmygodOhmyodOhmygod," I would whisper as an oncoming car veered too close to the center of the road.

"Concentrate on the scenery," Ali would say, and I would try to stare out the passenger window, improving my reading comprehension by deciphering the Farsi shop signs and billboards. But before long, I was back at it, imagining a cosmic comeuppance with every semi that whooshed past.

For someone with my overactive imagination, even the country roads were perilous. But in the summer of 1972, my first summer in Iran, I had resolved to mend my irritating ways. My husband had just completed his first year of teaching and research at the University of Tehran, where he had dreamed of teaching since he was a teenager, so we decided to celebrate by taking a trip to Mashhad, 550 miles northeast of Tehran. On this trip, I had willed myself not to worry about the traffic or the potholed, winding roads, or fate. Even I was tired of hearing my own protestations. We were on vacation, and both Ali and I needed a break from my fears.

Our traveling companion was a family friend, also named Ali. (Traveling with two Alis was not at all confusing to me, but it might be for a reader, so I'll refer to the Ali in the back seat as Ali J. I'm using his initial to be safe. After 43 years, it's likely that the statute of limitations, if there is still such a thing in Iran, has run out long ago, but one can never be sure.) Ali J. was one of the first friends I made in Tehran. He had graduated from high school a few years before and was trying to go abroad to study engineering. He liked to practice his English on me, and he was patient with my Persian. Charming and handsome, he was the perfect traveling companion; he had a laconic sense of humor and was a great storyteller—just the person to take my mind off the road.

The third-hand, 1960s-vintage blue Volvo my brother-in-law found for us had been a taxi in a previous life. Soon after we got it, I made Ali remove the telltale string of garish multi-colored lights festooned under the dashboard. I appreciated folk art and Iranian kitsch, but those taxi lights were too proletarian, even for an idealistic, democratic-socialist, university professor and his like-minded wife.

The car was all we could afford on a professor's salary. Only one of the Volvo's four tires was new; the treads on the others were worn out. The Alis decided to put their trust in fate—and the new tire. "It's 25% certain we won't have a flat," announced Ali J. But on the way to Mashhad, we did have a flat—and it was the new tire that blew out. By some divine miracle, the bald tires performed valiantly.

A little further on our journey, the radiator pipes burst. Since we didn't need a heater in summer, the Alis cut out the heater pipes and attached them to the radiator. But when Ali turned on the ignition, the radiator flooded the car. The Alis fixed that, too. I don't remember just how, but I think a pair of pantyhose was involved.

In Mashhad, we stayed with Ali J.'s sister and his brother-in-law, who had been my Ali's high school classmate in Kerman and later at the College of Agriculture in Karadj. Iranians are universally generous hosts, but Kermanis are particularly gracious. We were treated to trips to the bazaar, sumptuous lunches of herbed pilafs, kebabs, and braised chicken—most everything laced with saffron from the fields of nearby Gonabad. The languid days were punctuated with long naps, periodic cups of tea and slices of sweet, pale green *kharbozeh* melons for which Khorassan Province is famous. I understood why, when my sister-in-law made her annual pilgrimage to the shrine of Imam Reza in the heart of Mashhad, she always made sure to go when *kharbozeh* was in season.

We had not come to make a pilgrimage, but our hosts insisted that we couldn't leave Mashhad without visiting the shrine of Imam Reza, the eighth of the twelve Shi'ite Imams and the only one buried in Iran. For centuries, Shi'ites have traveled to the shrine to ensure their place in heaven. I was worried that I, a non-Moslem, wouldn't be allowed into the shrine, but Ali J.'s sister lent me a *chador*, and I joined the wave of pilgrims, ten-deep, as they circled the tomb. Her husband ran interference, walking backward with his arms outstretched protectively. A few of the pilgrims worked their way to the center to tie scraps of cloth, representing prayers or knotty problems, to the tomb's golden grillwork. Some believe that when the Imam intercedes and a problem is solved, the knots untie themselves. In my borrowed *chador*, I felt like an interloper, but I loved the simplicity of those scraps of cloth. I imagined the knotted scraps, their work done, flying open and drifting to the ground.

Too soon, it was time to make the ten-hour trip back to

Tehran. To ensure our safe return home, Ali J.'s sister prepared a tray with a glass of lemon sharbat, pastries, and the Holy Koran and held it above our heads as we made our way out of the house. Ali J. had his own prescription for the dangers of the road. He told my Ali, "If we have an accident, in a village or on the road, just keep going, because the villagers will kill us first and ask questions later."

We had been travelling for about two or three hours through the countryside when we saw a village teahouse in the distance and next to it a small *gendarmerie*, or police station. Large trucks were parked on either side of the two-lane road, big Mercedes-Benz semis and smaller, wooden trucks with colorful floral or geometric designs, some sporting names of the Imams, others with turquoise beads to ward off the evil eye. On the opposite side of the road, families had spread tablecloths on a grassy slope for late afternoon tea. Children were in motion everywhere, happy to be let out of their cars to run free in the cool grass. As Ali slowly navigated between the rows of trucks, I noticed a young boy running down the hill toward the road. For a tenth of a second my mind automatically triangulated the distance between the boy on the hill, our approaching car, and the crowded roadside. In that tenth of a second, I imagined him running in front of our car.

Stop that! Do not think that way. No one will thank you for your overwrought imagination. The old Ellen would have yelled, "Watch out for that boy!" but this new, self-controlled Ellen calmly stared straight ahead, allowing herself to be borne forward through this clump of vehicles, happy to have averted another verbal confrontation with her husband.

In another tenth of a second there was a loud, dull thud and a spray of glass—then the sound of a child crying and then a high-pitched wail in the distance. An old man in a crocheted skullcap came running up to the car, followed by a wiry, gray-haired woman, her chador left behind, her thin, cotton, homemade dress clinging to her bony chest. Her mouth was a black slash, her wailing silent now.

"OhmygodOhmygodOhmygod," I screamed, this time with some justification.

"Are you OK?" Ali asked me. I nodded. I had a lapful of crushed glass, but I was all right. We both turned back to look at Ali J., who was brushing little glass pebbles out of his hair, but otherwise unscathed.

Just outside the car, we saw a little boy, about nine years old clutching his head and screaming. It was the same boy I had seen at the top of the grassy hill. That hill was now empty of picnickers. They had all gathered around our car.

"Remember what I told you," said Ali J., but my Ali got out of the car, and Ali J. and I had no choice but to follow him.

"*Khak too saram!* Dirt on my head! *Bebakshid, Agha.* Forgive us, sir," the old man said, nodding in Ali's direction. "This donkey boy of ours! He never listens…always running…."

The woman whispered prayers as she held a piece of flowered cloth to the boy's bleeding head. Aside from the blood, the frightened boy seemed to be intact, although we couldn't be sure. He was screaming too loudly to question him.

From the corner of my eye, I saw an abandoned knife on a wooden table. I hoped no one else had seen it. The crowd pressed closer, everyone talking at once. Then, they were quiet. From the edge of the crowd, one voice prevailed. "What happened here?" It was a young *gendarme* from across the road.

"We were going very slowly," my Ali explained, "when all of a sudden this boy here darted out from between these trucks and ran right into our car. He must have hit his head on the wind wing," he said, gesturing toward the triangular window jutting out at a right angle on the passenger side, shards of glass still clinging to its frame. People in the crowd nodded in agreement. *That's the way it happened. It was the kid's fault. Praise be to God it's nothing worse.*

Seeing that our car was blocking traffic, Ali J. moved the Volvo to an empty spot alongside the road. Thinking Ali J. may have been the driver or maybe just wanting to use him as collateral, two older gendarmes arrived and took him into custody.

"I'm going to have to file a report," the young gendarme said to my Ali.

"Of course. But first this boy needs to see a doctor."

"Shouldn't we call an ambulance?" I asked.

"*Khanom*, there's no ambulance around here," said someone in the crowd.

"It'll be faster if you take him yourself," said another.

"The nearest doctor is about 15 miles away," said the young *gendarme*, "but I can't let you go alone. I'll have to go with you."

So, as Ali J. was led off to the *gendarmerie*, Ali and I brushed the glass off the back seat of our little Volvo, and the young *gendarme* slid in beside the boy and his father.

Once on the road, the boy continued to whimper and the old man fingered his worry beads.

"What's your name, *Agha*," asked Ali.

"Moghadas, *Agha*. Mohammad-e Moghadas." His family name meant "holy."

"And your boy?"

"Hassan."

Hassan-e Moghadas. Holy Hassan. *Holy Hassan! What a road trip this is turning out to be.*

It was dark when we reached the nearest town. The clinic was closed, but the gendarme directed us to the doctor's house on a tidy, tree-lined street in a middleclass neighborhood. We waited under a streetlamp while Ali went up to the gate and rang the bell. There was no answer, but we could hear the scuffing of slippers and the rattle of tea glasses from the courtyard behind the high wall. "Is anybody home?" Ali shouted over the wall. "We need a doctor, here."

"Go away," a man answered. "It's late."

"We have a little boy here. He's been hurt."

"The clinic opens at nine."

"Please, *Agha-ye Doktor*," shouted the *gendarme*. "It's me, Sergeant Khalili. Excuse me, but there's been an accident. With your permission sir, this little boy is bleeding. We would be your servants if Your Excellency would--if it is not too much trouble--be so kind as to bring his ceremony down here and attend to this child."

There was no answer, just the sound of slippers scuffing into the house. At last, the door opened and a scowling, pajama-clad doctor stepped out onto his porch and surveyed our anxious little group in the street below. "What's the problem?"

We steered Hassan under the streetlamp so the gash on his head would be visible.

"Eh, Baba," the doctor said from the top of the stairs, "worse things happen to people, and they don't bother to come to the doctor!"

I had had enough. "You're a doctor, aren't you?" I said, summoning my meager Persian. "Didn't you take an oath? You need to look at this child. There might be glass in his wound."

Whichever did the trick--the reminder of the Hippocratic oath or the embarrassment of having a foreign woman remind him--the doctor relented and motioned Hassan and his father inside. Ali and I waited outside, under the glow of the streetlamp and the vigilant gaze of the *gendarme*.

About fifteen minutes later, Agha-ye Moghadas and young Hassan emerged, the latter sporting a large gauze bandage. Ali paid the doctor, and we all piled back in the car. We were all relieved that Hassan's wound was superficial and hadn't required stitches. All that was left for us was to find a pharmacy and fill the prescription the doctor had written.

On the way back to the *gendarmerie*, the old man was still apologizing for the trouble his son had caused us. "Wait a minute," said the *gendarme*, "you can press charges, you know." *Yes, there was money to be made here*, I thought. *A university professor fresh from America, an American wife? What an opportunity! Let's not be rash, Agha-ye Moghadas!* With the *gendarme's* ministrations, we had no idea what we would be in for when we returned to the *gendarmerie*.

While we were dealing with the doctor, Ali J. was busy at the gendarmerie using his considerable charm to convince his captors not to put handcuffs on him. However, he couldn't dissuade them from putting him in a cell. He sat there alone, listening to the crowd outside, their collective mumbling sounding to him like a lynch mob in an American Western. The *gendarmes* had taken his identity card, and he feared he would never get it back, would never be able to get a passport to study abroad.

After a while, Ali J. was taken to the Chief Sergeant, who told him that all three of us would have to spend the night in jail and wait for the judge to arrive the next day. "Who are you?" he shouted. "And who is that foreign woman. What is she doing with you?"

Here is where Ali J. took his ingenuity to a level even higher than the one that allowed him to repair the broken radiator. "Actually, this American lady has been invited by Her Majesty Shahbanou Farah to assist with a major art project. And the man who was driving her? Well, sir, that's her husband, a famous scientist from America who has been invited by His Majesty the Shahanshah himself to teach at the university." The more Ali J. embellished his story, the calmer and friendlier the Chief Sergeant became.

"You know, I'm really getting hungry," said Ali J., although food was the last thing on his mind. To show that he had money, he pulled out a 100-toman bill and laid it on the Chief Sergeant's desk. "I don't want to eat alone. Won't you join me?" The Chief Sergeant sent one of his men to the village *chello kebabi* to buy dinner for everyone. Ali, tapping even deeper into his talents as a yarn spinner, commiserated with the Chief Sergeant on his tribulations and heavy responsibilities because he himself had relatives who were army generals.

When the Chief Sergeant sent for Hassan's mother and other relatives who were waiting nearby and proceeded to harangue them for letting Hassan, that *haramzade* (bastard) child, disrupt the plans of the royal family, Ali J. knew he had succeeded.

As soon as we arrived at the *gendarmerie* with Hassan, Ali J. told my Ali about the story he had concocted. Ali gave some money to the Chief Sergeant and Hassan's parents, and we were free to go. The *gendarmes* took our addresses in case there were any further problems. The Chief Sergeant gave his name to Ali J. and asked if, in the future, he might put in a good word with one of his army general relatives to get him a promotion.

Eventually, I learned to drive, and I learned not to second-guess myself. I learned when to be silent and when to speak up. I'm still a nervous passenger, but I have developed a useful shorthand. When Ali is driving and I see a potential accident, all I need to say is, Hassan-e Moghadas! Holy Hassan!

Nan Friedley

It came in the mail

on Tuesday
mixed in with the Penny Saver
weekly grocery ads and gas bill
an innocent-looking envelope
carelessly I tear it open

a single page
an obituary…mine
stamped with *draft* copy
a mistake?
birth date, place of birth
education, work experiences
next of kin…all correct
my journey reduced
to one piece of paper
date of death—ten days from today
like expiration on a milk carton

> I have until a week from Friday
> to edit my life story
> return it for *final* publication
> to a P.O. box

it becomes apparent
that each event hinges on
a previous one
friends not met
from jobs I never had
unborn daughter

from a nonexistent marriage

ten days is not enough
I initial *no change*

Nan Friedley

elusive perfect fit

I unwrap the tissue
like layers of an onion
see strings not yet laced
waiting

to be worn out of the store
walk with a swagger
parade them in front of friends
ideal shoes

flaunt them every day
avoid sticky gum, jealous puddles
tiptoe around trouble spots
protect my sole

but soon they rub
cause blisters
lose their luster
tongues wag, laces fray
between narrowed eyes

return them to the box
in the back of the closet

like the stepsisters
a match meant for someone else

Window #3

Weaving through the maze
of customers cashing paychecks
I'm calculating which
teller will serve me.

Beanie, welding goggles
neon yellow vest:
my construction worker disguise.

Next

I slide my block- printed note
to teller of window #3
    THIS IS A ROBBERY
    NO TRACKING DEVICE
    COMPLY WITH MY WISHES
    I HAVE A GUN
                 My training kicks in.
                 Just stay calm.
Give me the money in the top drawer.
                 I pull it open, stacking the contents
                 taking note of his tattoos
                 slipping the tracker into the fifties bundle.

Now the money in your bottom drawer.
                 I don't have a bottom drawer…a lie.

I'm not giving him $35,000.

I grab the bills
shoving them in my vest pocket
slowing my car
in a few blocks I toss
the concealed tracker
out the window.

Our FBI security guy
follows the blip online
then it stops.
Oh well, by sticking in that tracker
I was gifted $500.
"Thank you, Security Pacific".

Nan Friedley

Captivity

he captured her
one sultry August evening
making a bed of
twigs and leaves
in a mayonnaise jar
with a nail-hole lid
screwed on tightly

she eyed her captor
fluttered wildly
in her see-through prison

he watched as she
illuminated,
green intervals...on...off
until her light dimmed
trapped under glass
leaving the dark

Nan Friedley

Predators

friendless except for each other
they search the playground
circling the tetherball court
holding hands
whispering conspirators
products of abuse
from similar dysfunctional homes
looking for their next victim
an easy target separated
from the herd, vulnerable
who might even cry
from their taunts and barks

fat girl, always ripe
skinny, frail boy
malnourished self-esteem
geek with glasses
reading a book alone

retarded kid
too easy

but the bell rings
leaving them to attack another day
slinking back to their classes' line
like lonely wolves
blending in with the pack

Nan Friedley

Aimless

in Target's parking lot
pushing the key fob's
red triangle
hoping my nondescript gray car
will sound the alarm
I'm over here

but it's the busiest
shopping day of the year
with an infinite
sea of gray sedans
wearing grills like grins

passing by the same
gray Honda Civic
for the third time
wish I could remember
which row
which side of the lot
wish I'd written it on my hand

others with an internal
parking lot GPS
are now watching
chuckling, shaking their heads
at my clueless self
loaded down with
shopping bags
wandering aimlessly

next time I'm buying
a bug-gut green Hummer

Nan Friedley

Critic at Friday Matinee

with a small tub of popcorn and soda
in hand she chooses a seat
half-way up on the aisle
during the twilight of commercials
before the previews begin
and darkness falls

no one to share popcorn
or conversation
she busies herself with
checking cell phone messages
sipping on her drink
turning to allow fellow moviegoers
entrance into the row

she could just as easily
watch on Netflix or Pay-Per-View
but the big-screen surround-sound
just-released teasers
for the latest action flick
beckon her to sit alone
in a dark theatre

as the end credits roll
she quickly makes her way to the exit
is she anxious
about being labeled
friendless, husband-less, family-less
just less

I watch alone from my aisle seat
two rows behind

Nan Friedley

Nutri-Ninja with Ultra IQ™

super extractor extraordinaire
more than a blender
faster than a speeding bullet
more powerful than a locomotive
even sounds like a freight train
rumbling through my kitchen

googling smoothie recipes
exploring Pinterest
for ones that detox
protein-replacement meals
anti-oxidant, vitamin-packed
juices to make me "glow"

special trip to Sprouts
in search of chia seeds
wondering if I consume them
will I become a living Chia Pet
when nourished with coconut water

layering ingredients
kale, celery, apples, blueberries, ice
whirred together in 45 seconds
brain freeze drinking too fast
45 seconds later

I should feel wonderful
rejuvenated by the blast
of healthy fruits and veggies

but my teeth yearn
for something to chew
my jaw has atrophied
I lust for crunch

Françoise Frigola

Going with the flow

As we are taught,
it is so important to go with the flow,
to let it go through me.

What other choice do I have?

None.

Incontinence offers no option!

Françoise Frigola

Succession

three trees
motionless

the sound of the wind

the farthest tree shakes its branches
like wings
then stops

the middle tree, in turn,
agitates its long green needles
then pauses

the closest tree
starts its own dance
then rests

I now feel the wind caressing my face.

Françoise Frigola

Decisions-Decisions-Decisions: Musings on Artistic Choices

Why?

Are you sure this is the right thing to do?

Sometimes the answer is a clear YES! Other times, there is no clear answer.

What choice is better than the other? Why is this better than that? Is this one really better? How will I know until I try?

As a child, when I made what my mother considered the "wrong" decision, I was always blamed because I should have thought of the consequences. I should have known better!

In retrospect, in most cases, as a child, how the heck could I have known what would result from a simple decision or action?

This concept of having to know the result before even getting started was a hindrance for a long time, unless, I, somehow, knew which choice to make.

Years ago, I was hesitant about getting into a new relationship. My therapist had the magic words: "How would you know unless you try?" These words were so healing!

They have now become part of my decision process: make the best possible choice given what I know and go for it until I realize, if needed, that this was the wrong choice or that I need to make modifications of some types.

There is, however, one area in my life where I change my mind a lot: it is during the so-called "creative process," in this case, visual art.

Usually, I start a piece of art with something in mind. Along the way, however, new ideas, new concepts, new directions emerge. I pick one, move on, only to be flooded by new ones. Sometimes I stay on the same track, most often I do not.

Ma favorite art medium is one in which I do not have much control over the process. Along the way, there are many decisions to make, of course, but they simply flow, especially when I have very little time to make such a decision. A typical example is when I sculpt with acrylic sheets. When it is heated at two hundred degrees Fahrenheit, with three layers of gloves on each hand, I have to quickly and carefully grab it. I have only a few seconds to give it a shape before it cools off and turns rigid again. In most cases, the piece does not shape itself exactly the way I had envisioned. In these few seconds, I feel I am making millions of decisions.

The ultimate decision is when to stop working on the artwork: when is a piece of art complete?

Many years ago, I engraved my own version of a Native American pictograph on a clear acrylic sheet. Imitating the technique used thousands of years ago in petroglyphs, I reproduced the image with a Dremmel tool by carving tiny cupules close to each other. Once the image was finished, I took a few steps back to look at it and loved the result: tiny white round half-spheres on the clear background.

In my heart, I wanted to keep it this way. I also knew that it would sell better if it had color.

What a difficult decision to make!

White on a clear background gave the artwork its "potential." It was like a black and white photograph versus a color one. The viewer has to participate, to project oneself into the image to see it.

I knew that, as soon as I would put one drop of color, all possibilities would be forever lost. I would lock the artwork onto itself without any possibility, any hope of change. I was freezing it rather than giving it life with its endless opportunities.

I carefully decided on browns, oranges, yellows, and reds. Before starting, however, I had the idea of filling the two bottom rows of cupules with deep purple. The viewer would never notice, unless choosing to carefully examine each color. Yet, that tiny change, made all the difference in the final artwork.

This was the inspiration which, for me, "saved" the sculpture, the concept that kept it alive even though I froze it forever by applying colors.

This was a challenging decision!

The result was quite positive: the first person who saw the artwork bought it!

Françoise Frigola

My Friend the Tree

We met
Some twenty years ago, during one of my walks, in the forest,
behind my house.

The mountainside was steep.
From above, I could admire his majesty, yet he was quite
humble.
He was healthy, in his prime.
He was surrounded by various trees and shrubs, such that
many animals -
Especially squirrels, jumping from branch to branch - were
constantly visiting him.
He was the center of life in this corner of the forest.

I approached him, touched his bark. I felt at home.
I wanted to hug him, but the amount of resin told me he did
not want me to be so close.

I climbed the trail back up a bit and sat on the rugged slope
to have a full view.
Then the conversation began.

And thereafter, whenever I had the energy, I would walk to
him, sit down, and listen.
Often, I would ask for guidance in my life and then wait for
an answer. The wisdom always came.

Our exchanges continued for many months.
They had to do with my health and its unknown, my feeling of

isolation from the world.

His wisdom and his joy for life were powerfully contagious and helped me continue to survive.

Then we experienced the Bee Canyon fire.

While I had evacuated, knowing the fire was moving close to my house, I often thought of him: was he still alive? Would he survive?

When I returned, bulldozers were actively destroying the forest, creating a thirty-foot wide protective perimeter. I know it was supposed to be for our safety, but my heart was hurting for all the trees, bushes, grass, totally destroyed - not to mention the insects, birds, rats, mice, and other animals whose habitat was being condemned.

The ground was bare, totally bare.

As soon as I could, I rushed to visit my friend.

The sight devastated to my heart.

The bulldozers had not touched him, but had cleared everything around him.

He was now standing all alone, without any connections to any of the other trees or shrubs.

All the time I was with him, I could not see any animals visiting him.

Could I ever relate to his situation!

He was very sad, but decided to survive anyway, at least, live his life the best he could, all alone, totally cut off from the rest of the forest, from the rest of his world.

Months went by.

The piles of dead wood from the clearing were becoming a fire hazard, so it was decided to burn them.

As much as I trusted the firefighters who were supervising these huge fires, these gigantic flames made me very nervous, especially because they were so close to larges trees in general, and to my friend in particular. Just the heat itself was unbearable for me, so how was it for him?
I was not alone, so I could not ask him. I told him I would be back as soon as I could.

I kept my promise and came back two days later.

As soon as I turned the corner of the trail, my heart broke: his needles, usually so green and shiny, had turned greenish-grey.

Could it be?
Could it be that my friend had given up?
Could it be that isolation, then intense heat, plus the total lack of consideration from those who set up the fires, were too much for him?

Could I be wrong?
Could it just be the light making his needles look grey?

I asked and listened attentively, but did not get any answer.
I came back the next day.
Now his needles were definitely grey.
No doubt, my friend was dying if not already dead.
I sobbed and sobbed and sobbed.

The human attacks had been too much for him.
He just could not make it.
It was way too hard.

He chose to quit.

I felt strongly that the heat of the fire so close to him was only a small part of his demise, that it was the straw that broke the camel's back. I felt and knew that the isolation, the lack of connection with Life, were the deepest issue.

And again, I sobbed, and sobbed, and sobbed.

About a week later, his needles were brown; then they turned pale grey, almost white.

Later, he was considered a fire hazard and cut down.
Gone forever.

A few weeks ago, eighteen years later, for my birthday, I decided to go back to the same area.
No trace of my tree at all.
However, the bare ground of clearing is now filled with beautiful, young, and healthy six-foot-high manzanitas.
The so-called mountain lilacs are even higher.

Life is back.
Nature has rejuvenated itself.

My friend, the tree, is still alive in my memory, and especially in my heart.
I will not give in to isolation.
Contrary to my friend the tree, I can always reach out and not be alone.

Françoise Frigola

Dancing Shadows

light, will you stop moving?
you make my head spin!

you are showing me way too many shadows!
are you trying to tell me something?

what are you saying?
you are dancing?
dancing?

oh I get it!
dancing shadows!

yes, of course.
thank you
for the reminder
how long has it been?
when did we start?
if I recall correctly,
it was in the late 80's
yes, indeed,
an acrylic sculpture
alone at home,
I had worked on it the whole day
two beings
almost stick figures
more or less looking like people

I had put them in the oven
to soften the plastic
I was just about to pull them out

when I heard a key in the door
no! I thought!
I want to be alone to finish that piece.
I always want to be alone when I do my art.
I only had a minute
I pulled the two figures out of the oven
hoping they would be hot enough
to be shaped
with three pairs of gloves on
I took them in my hands
and, somehow,
as if by themselves
they took shape
almost merged
into one another
holding each other tight
I was amazed
not what I had planned
but,
I never had any clear plan
they came to life
as if by themselves
one white
one black
dancing
Dancing Shadows

Marie Griffiths

Winter Sheets: a Prose Poem in Two Voices

Momma:

January and another laundry day in Maine, no use complaining, your very bones know the recipe for winter sheets . . . roll old Maytag across scuffed linoleum and plug cord into outlet. Hook up hose to faucet. Fill, distributing wash for balance. Shake in Lux soap flakes. (Sip a cup of tea and dream a little while machine churns). Detach hose and drain into sink. Haul up each sodden sheet, feed through wringer. Stay alert now! (That devil wringer has a mind of its own; thwacked your tummy once and lost what would have been a baby boy). Fill machine again, adding Mrs. Stewart's bluing to rinse water. Repeat wringer step.

As carefully as folding Old Glory, gather edges together, pleat every sheet, piling wicker basket high. Stop to dress in woolen coat with faux fur collar, calf length rubber boots, kerchief. Ice-crusted snow underfoot, lug load to clothes line. Wooden peg-style pins stuffed in pockets, an extra clenched between teeth, hoist a sheet. Starting with one end, jam down a pin. Unfurl next section. Jam again. Fingers numb and first sheet stiff before last is hung, all in rigor mortis under a pallid sun. Never mind, sheets just have to get done.

Her Daughter:

Bitterly cold, not wickedly as we are prone to say these days. So bitter, Momma, still a novice driver, was moved to collect me from school. Before leaving she'd noted her laundry's still frozen condition, but a freshening breeze was swinging sheets with some vigor, perhaps would thaw them a mite. Momma drove fastidiously, (tended to ride the clutch). Allowing herself a short sigh of relief, she pulled our 1951 Plymouth sedan into the drive without mishap.

What *was* that apparition scudding white on white in the fading light? And there went another. "Jesus, Mary and Joseph," her only exclamation, we skated, chasing trapezoids and rhombi lashed along by preamble of a nor'easter. Dampness in the dining room followed. Chairs draped in limp white resembled a Bar Harbor hotel at summer season's closing. Finally, a sizzling iron and the clean perfume of winter sheets.

Dedicated to Development by the North Fontana Planning Committee

And if they are sad about how they must ... die,
perhaps it is our vocation to be their regret.
Rainer Marie Rilke
Sonnets to Orpheus, XIV

Late winter in the Cucamonga Valley,
and rows of grapevines, shaped like warped,
wrought-iron candelabra, vanish
at the concrete horizon of the I-15North.
Just beyond, easterly peaks of the San Gabriels
loom, backdrop to vineyard drama.

Decades of bonsai-like pruning yet
these vines endure, trunks grotesque,
branches bent as a crone's back.
February, now, and still black as if burnt
by last summer's sun, they are starkness
in a blowing, yellow sea of mustard weed.

For, finally, rain has come in a drought year.
Mustard thrives, but vines hardly notice.
Blind moles nosing aside stones, their roots
have probed through alluvium, year
after year downwards, at last tapping
the sustaining aquifer.

Such tortuous, stunted vines never were
staked straight, trellised like younger

cousins in Napa and Sedona.
For nearly a hundred winters, these dormant,
silent companions in the wind have dreamt
of a purple harvest.

Soon, like some Biblical miracle of fertility,
venerable cordons will bring forth delicate,
chartreuse leaves, and canes will bud. Yet,
these final thousand acres are fated
to be sundered. Fontana's dowagers have born
their last cluster of sweet, sweet grapes.

Marie Griffiths

Prayer to Saint Patrick from an Aspiring American Writer

I beseech thee, where is that famed silver tongue,
the Irish storyteller in me? Far removed
from the land of bogs and faeries, Gaelic
blood still flows in these veins.

Perhaps I am descendent from dull
potato eaters, peat cutters muttering
into pewter flagons at the village pub,
or woollen-shawled women gathering
seaweed to amend impoverished soil,
shrill-voiced, selling cockles on market day.

Perhaps one of these stowed away in steerage
and not a Corkonian chit of sixteen,
her native wit sharp-whittled in convent school.
Not that same Nora daily passing Blarney Castle
and its stone, caring not a whit for relics
but dreaming of a brasher land.

To be sure, no Yeats or Heaney in my lineage
but there was bespectacled Nana.
The long plaited hair of her youth, gone white
as hoarfrost, she would dandle me on a knee
in rhythm to the lyrics of Tennyson's "Lady of Shallot,"
recited line after rote-learned line.

Saint Patrick, who rid Erin of its snakes,
rid me of impediment. Please, set my pen free.

Teresa Halliburton

All True-istic

Light blue sky

Bright white disc

Shooting star

Make a wish

Not for self

Others welfare

Learn and teach

Compassion and care

Teresa Halliburton

Mystic Flight

We take the path of stillness
And later may come to move
Spontaneous with no mind
It's how we find our groove

Hard work every single day
When done right, it feels like play
Some will move using thinking
But, this is not our linking

Peaceful mind and peaceful heart
Will calibrate a new start
Almost anyone can heal
You can also learn to feel

Teresa Halliburton

Drop By Drop

From the house of mirror neurons
I feel your pain I do

When we marry in the moment
Our empathy comes through

We don't have to think about it
It's natural for a few

We all train our nervous system
The same but different is true

So how we mold our character
Dictates the energy we imbue

Everything then is cumulative
And we are nourished by the dew

Teresa Halliburton

A Zensational Push

I have lived in the Chinese Room for years
Beyond all my expectations and fears
past culture and thinking
and new way of linking
Consciousness and movement are sent
Vibration
Translation
With no mind
We may find
Our true self
and good health

Teresa Halliburton

A New Vernacular

Mentess, Momtor
Here are words for

Women guiding
Us through our life

And helping us
In times of strife

Mentess, Momtor
Use these, either or

Teresa Halliburton

I Held A Hummingbird

I held a hummingbird
You can believe my word
Massage was unfinished
My body unblemished
Anna flew in to see
What's going on with me
She went to the window
Then could no further go
I held fingers to help
Mounted without a yelp
She stood on my right hand
As if it had been planned
I took her to the door
And she flew some more
I held a hummingbird
You can believe my word

Teresa Halliburton

Living The Life

In Art
There are no rules

In Music
Play what you feel

In Poetry
Say what you think

In Love
This makes you real

Teresa Halliburton

The Mind Of The Cosmos

10 x 108
The universe is alive
A quantum computer
With bees in a hive

Ultimate organism
Promoting life
Cosmos brain
Transmuting strife

Complex programs
Simple codes
Patterns of atoms
History of nodes

See the past
And future too
Fractal geometry
Gives a clue

We are the optimal scientists
Exploring experiments in space
Asking questions of this life
With the answers showing on our face

A living machine
Or created dream
Our conscious participation
With biological computation

Teresa Halliburton

Relative Opinions

Who can say how
high is high
What is what
why is why

Only me and
only you
Say it is
know it's true

Allow for each
to believe
See ideas
and conceive

Teresa Halliburton

Bridge In The Rain

There was a horizontal bridge for peasants
Being trafficked by local poor residents

Rebuilt bamboo over centuries
Afford familial luxuries

Along this over water road
They carried a heavy load

Coming and going: arms, carts full
Everyone knows this is the rule

As far as every monsoon season goes
It is as if the sky was a non-stop hose

Many colored hats and umbrellas
Keeping covered gals and young fellas

Out above the ocean stories high
Normally only small children cry

Running faster than ever before
Trying to see who's first at the shore

Whenever the rain comes down
There's rarely a frown

Elders set a good example
They show laughter can be ample

Snuffy

It was summer of the year 2000. I started to notice that a dirty brown dog was always running through our yard. We saw lots of stray dogs, but only once, as they traveled through on their way to someplace more interesting. This dog was skinny, his bones sticking out, his long spindly legs wobbling as he walked, and his back legs bowed out like an old cowpoke. The ends of his toes on the right front paw were missing. After a few weeks I realized that the dog was actually living in our yard.

No matter how ugly he was, I could not let a living creature starve outside our kitchen door. I started putting out food and water for the dog. He wouldn't come within 30 feet of me, though he stared at the dish intently. As soon as I returned to the house, he was instantly there, wolfing down everything.

As the days and weeks rolled by I became fascinated by the dog. It dawned on me that the rustling and snuffling I heard at night was the dog, sleeping under the bushes right outside our bedroom window. It was a damp, cold place, and I couldn't understand why a poor creature would sleep in such an inhospitable location. Could it possibly be that there was some comfort in being near us?

I began to want a relationship with this dog. There was something about his diffidence that made me want to win him over. Why was that? I had always hated dogs as a child. I despised their slavish desire for human affection. On some level, it felt way too much like my own neediness. But this dog wanted nothing to do with our affection. That was a challenge.

I remembered a story, a Korean folktale about a woman whose loving husband was sent off to war. When he returned he no longer smiled. He refused her embraces and would not look her in the eye. He never spoke. When all her efforts to regain their former tenderness had failed, she consulted a magician.

"Please give me a potion to make my husband love me again," she pleaded.

The magician promised to do so. "But the potion will only work," he told her, "if you bring me three hairs from a tiger's whiskers."

"A tiger's whiskers! The tiger will kill me first!"

"That is your challenge," the magician replied.

The woman went home and thought about what to do for a long time. Then one day she went deep into the forest where the tiger lived. In a clearing she unwrapped a large, fresh piece of meat, placed it on the ground and retreated far away, where she climbed a tree to watch what would happen. Eventually a tiger smelled the meat, came to the clearing, and devoured it. Then he left. The woman returned to the clearing every day with fresh meat. Each day the tiger ate and left. After a few weeks, trembling all over, she climbed down from the tree, stood next to its massive trunk and let the tiger see her watching him as he ate. He looked up, but his hunger satisfied, he turned and left. A few weeks after that, she took one step closer to the tiger. After a few more weeks she took another step. After many months, she was able to stand right in front of the tiger as he ate the fresh meat. She slowly reached into her pocket and pulled out a tiny pair of scissors. Leaning forward, lightly stroking the tiger's head, she gently snipped three hairs from the tiger's whiskers.

The next day she returned to the magician.

"I've brought three hairs from a tiger's whiskers! Now you can make the potion so my husband will love me again!"

She carefully drew the hairs from a small leather bag and handed them to the magician. He took the hairs and, with barely a glance, tossed them into the fire.

"What have you done!" she cried. "Do you know how long it took me to get those whiskers?" The magician looked at her, smiled, and slowly spoke these words.

"You no longer need the tiger's whiskers. All you need is to do with your husband what you did with that tiger."

I decided to put this story's lesson to the test...with the dog.

Each morning and evening I put out fresh food and water for the dog. I spoke to him kindly. He stayed far away and ventured closer only when I had returned to the house. He barked for hours at night. He woke us up so many times that we got a noisy fan for the bedroom. We ran the fan every night to drown out the intermittent, ragged din.

We called him Dog Boy, not yet ready to give him a name of his own.

But as the months went by, and we read the Harry Potter Books aloud to each other at night, we settled on the name Snuffy, partly short for Snuffles, the dog name of Harry's godfather Sirius Black, and partly for the fact that he often made a snuffling sound as he warily eyed us, ready to run from under the hanging branches of the pepper tree outside the sliding glass doors in the kitchen.

I came across a journal entry from October 1, 2000, the other day. It read, "Our little goofy dog came up to me today a little happy, a tiny bit enthusiastic – made me so hopeful. This is such a gripping drama for me – trying to win the affection of that unattainable being." And so it went, very slowly.

A month later on November 21, 2000, I wrote, "Snuffy is so sad. I wish I knew what was the very best thing to do for his happiness." My dream was that one day Snuffy would let me pat him on the head, pet him, even wrap my arms around his neck and give him a tender hug.

It was actually a year and a half before he would even let me lightly touch him on the head.

Snuffy could climb a chain link fence, and he often climbed over ours to meet with his friends next door, the two German Shepherds, Bert and Bonnie. They were both taller and more massive than Snuffy's slender 50 pounds, but the three of them ran around in the yard together and never fought. Our neighbors, however, hated Snuffy, especially his all-night barking, and his forays into their back yard. One day, two years later, they called to say they would shoot him if he came onto their property one more time. We had to enlist the aid of animal control to capture Snuffy. Then we took the big leap and got him to a trainer, a devotee of the Strict, Highly Structured, Extremely Controlling School of dog handlers. We knew nothing about schools or how to train dogs and listened to everything she said. She took Snuffy for two weeks. She later told us he was so riddled with fleas that they had embedded themselves deep into his flesh. Her team had to wash him over and over. I can't even imagine how agonizing that must have been for this extremely skittish dog. He came home looking even more anxious and fearful, but he was clean and beautiful, he could walk on a leash and sit on command. This meant that we now had to become real, committed dog owners, rather than feral dog food providers.

This was an extremely difficult period for Snuffy and for us. None of us knew how to be a dog family. The trainer told us Snuffy must be under control at all times, either in a crate all night, walking on a leash with us, or locked inside a kennel in the back yard. He hated the leash but reluctantly let us walk him, though he cowered and quivered at every car or human being that passed. Now my husband and I were as anxious as Snuffy. We tried to do what the trainer wanted, even when it just didn't feel right and Snuffy looked at us with pleading, anxious eyes, one ear standing up and the other flopped over, as if exhausted by our "no's" and "stop pulling!" One day we decided to take Snuffy to the dog park. Maybe he could actually have some fun and run free. He loved other dogs, and was never aggressive.

When we got there, the other dog owners said he had to come off the leash to enter the park. Could Snuffy handle this? Would he come back when called? This seemed doubtful. My husband said, "Don't let him off the leash. Let's just go." But in that moment something broke free inside of me. I couldn't take it any more, all the don'ts, the total lack of joy. With a sense of wild abandonment, casting aside all received wisdom, I let him off the leash.

Snuffy took one look at the other dogs, and without a glance back ran for the chain link fence, handily climbed it in seconds and was off into the rushes of the Santa Ana River bottom. We followed and called, but Snuffy was gone. We returned home, shell shocked, sad... and relieved. Our life could return to its pre-Snuffy quiet and simplicity. I looked for Snuffy every time I drove over the Santa Ana Riverbed from Rubidoux to Riverside. One day, I thought I saw him standing on the riverbank staring far off, motionless. I felt a stab of pain in my chest, but I did not want Snuffy back.

Then one day, about six weeks later, we received a telephone call. Someone in Jurupa Hills told us they had found our phone number on the tag of a stray dog. Snuffy had climbed their fence, run through the backyard and fallen into the swimming pool. If they hadn't been home, he would have surely drowned. Could we please come and pick up our dog?

With heavy hearts, we got into the car and drove over. We had to come to terms with the fact that Snuffy had been trying to find his way back to us. He was more than halfway home already. When we got there, he was lying in the front yard chained to a tree. I felt like a mom coming to bail her son out of jail. We looked at each other with mutual resignation. No joy on either side, just acceptance. Snuffy's tiny stump of a tail faintly, slowly, wagged. This was *our dog*.

But when Snuffy came home that day, the military school regime was over. No more being locked up in the kennel all day. If he wanted to run into the wild hills behind the house the way he did before that was fine with us. He could sleep outside in his Dogloo, except at night, when he slept in his crate next to our bed. At least we could spare the neighbors the nightly barking.

We put the leash on only when we walked together on the street with the cars. We eventually came to love our walks with Snuffy. We would wave to our neighbors as they drove by. They would call out, "Nice dog!" or "What a beautiful dog!" Strangely, Snuffy was a beautiful dog to us now. His black, brown and red, short coat gleamed in the sunlight. He did not look like any kind of dog breed I could identify, but I loved his black, shining eyes and gentle expression. He still did not like being touched, but would endure it for our sakes if we gave him a light pat on the head or the back. If we had visitors, he never came out of the bedroom. He cowered, nose to the floor, in his crate, the only place he seemed to feel safe in the house.

The years flew by. Eventually we adopted another wild, stray dog, Redbone, who had became Snuffy's closest pal on his forays into the wild hills behind the house. They played together, and we were treated to the heartwarming sight of Snuffy actually having fun. Redbone died of cancer in 2010, and another stray, our adored Sweet Pea, already injured when we took her in, died a year later.

By this time, Snuffy was at least fourteen years old. He couldn't walk on the street with us any more. His legs bothered him. The only outdoor activity he could still manage was to slowly struggle up the back hill and roam the small wild space from which he had emerged back in the summer of 2000. We walked up there together many times, and I took photos of Snuffy at the top of the ridge, staring far out over Rubidoux toward Corona. One day he was no longer able to struggle up the hill. That just about broke my heart.

A few nights later, before we went to sleep, I knelt down to say goodnight to Snuffy as he entered his crate. He paused and sat down on the rug. I slowly and carefully wrapped my arms around his shoulders, and Snuffy let me hug him for the very first time. That magician had been right.

The next day, November 30, 2012, Snuffy could no longer walk. We called the vet. Snuffy died quietly without pain, lying on the rug outside his crate as we knelt by his side saying our goodbyes and thanking him from the bottom of our hearts.

What were we thanking him for actually? I have thought about this many times since we lost our boy. Thanks to Snuffy, I now love all dogs. I feel close to them, treasure the opportunity to whisper in their ears and give them pats. Snuffy also gave my husband and me the experience of parenting, complete with anguish, joy, grief, anger, regret, and all the emotions both positive and negative that are just too complicated to name. In addition, Snuffy taught us that sometimes you have to just let a troubled little being be, and not try to fix him and make him perfect. He was perfect for us just as he was.

Michael Orlich

Into a life

It was the first time—
later than most
all-ready
age hardening and
first flower fading
in memory.

It was painful—
cutting deep
into a life untamed
leaving bare, wounds
raw remains—
dormant, potent, ready
to bloom and grow.

Michael Orlich

One Life (In Nine Acts)

Act One.
There was work already
and pain—but also fun
with buddies and brothers
race tracks and filling stations
farms, fields, good meals
and ma at the hub.

Act Two.
The work increased
but so did the rewards,
a time to enjoy
long cars, good grades
and sports teams—
toughness an asset
on the football field.

Act Three.
The grades and football
promised open doors
but reality required more
work instead;
so loyalty wrote letters
as green fields
gave way to army drab
to tanks and oil
steel and manhood.

Act Four.
A new starter, a home
with a woman to love
and to work for
and two little girls
yours yet strangely foreign
to your world
of tough survival.
You tried, you worked
you pushed on—
but sometimes over.

Act Five.
Older now and again
a father, of a boy
more familiar
source of pride and joy
but different still
in some ways
like his mother.

Act Six.
Saver, provider
no harder worker
now lying in bed
betrayed by flesh and blood
vessels that threatened
death, demanded change.

Act Seven.
Children gone
and finally
long work done;
no pipe, no wrench, no mill
no work buddies
fewer brothers left,
life begins again
with home and wife.

Act Eight.
But she is mortal, fragile
and seems to fly away
like the others, but stays
as you hold her closer
than ever before.
Stronger than ever too
you have less need
to be tough or right
or in control.
It is enough to love.

Act Nine.
It lies ahead
and what it holds
none know.
Perhaps an ending
long deferred
but surely
new beginnings.

Michael Orlich

Trans-plant

I did not give you life,
form your fruit,
sink your silent seed
in fertile soil.

You came to me
embodied, as a gift
fully formed of fragile
leaf and branch and root-
ed though not grounded.

I watered, watched, worried,
gave you sun and shade,
transplanted you
to give you space
to grow. I cared.

And now you've grown
and outgrown this place
of mine. I see
your need to be
and not to be confined
by what before protected.

You may not survive
the change—I know—
may not take root
in this hard world,
but this is your chance.

Be free and fight.
I will hope and care.

Jane O'Shields-Hayner

I Am from the Land of Infamy

I.
I am from the lands of infamy,
The land where lightening strikes
with the snake.

Where winds tear the mother from her love
And toss what remains over the greedy land,

Hatred spits its curse there,
In your face,
Without provocation
and the hard-baked earth lies angry,
sickened by cruelty
and shame.

2.
I am from the lands of, deep green forests,
From streams, running cold, beating
Rhymes on every stone
and rhythms
on the grasses
they brush
part,
and braid
on their way
to the sea.

3.
I am from marshes and ponds of black mud and green waters,

From orange salamanders gathered in wriggling collectives,
From the shadows of tales that travel dirt roads
and lead me to the comfort of having known them before.
I have lain before, on their cool shores,
I had no fear. I remember.

4.
I am from the land of the brave,
The land where six hundred centuries of peoples lived without
wars,
Without greed,
Where the conquerors claimed and occupied,
Where the innocent were slaves,
or ghosts,
Where the bloody land
cursed the stench of its killers,
And expelled them,
Only to see their return.

5.
I am from the land of the brave,
A droplet of progeny
Washed to shore by flooding rivers,
Carried by slow moving fogs,
That creep over the hills
and work their ways homeward,

Train whistles call,
louder on cold nights,

enchanting the children.

Coyotes howl with the sirens' screams.
And
Roadrunners stand at my door,
to stare at my face.

The king snake coils here
when the diamond snake rattles,
And the hawks swoop low
to watch me float,
A large insect,
on a small drop
of violet- blue water.

Marsha Schuh

Dreams and Their Antitheses

Oh death in life, the days that are no more.
                                   —Alfred Lord Tennyson

Each morning, that instant between

my flight above a galaxy of city lights

in a soft blue dress under bluer stars

and the sudden stab of memory.

Secret place of books and vinyl disks,

tchotchkes, aroma of cardamom and lilac,

fine-fringed table cloths, tell-me stories

in turtle time, traveling toward dawn.

Place of dreaming in straight-backed chairs,

listening to hymns on an old upright,

concertos on cellos, pianissimo rustling

of leaves, gathering themselves into piles.

That moment of bliss before now,

wedged in the sliver between forever

and the whine of alarm clocks and mowers,

the insipid taste of albumen on toast.

The Antique Mall

Wandering through a maze of stalls,

I try to imagine the lives of women

who served countless Sunday dinners

on these Blue Willow plates, who scooped

breakfast from chipped white egg cups,

sipped from cobalt blue goblets

or ruby thumb-print water glasses,

arranged bouquets in emerald hobnail vases

their depths smelling faintly of faded roses,

who embroidered dishtowels and dresser scarves

that still bear the scent of lavender.

I try to picture the housewives who hung

these Norman Rockwell prints in new maple frames,

now redolent of fusty attics,

who wore these pearls, chokers, rope necklaces,

clip on earrings, pop beads, and silver charms.

I try to conjure the children who played

with this Toni Doll, complete with sugar

"setting solution" and plastic curlers,

the Yellow Tonka trucks and Red Flyer wagon,

loaded with Etch-a-Sketch, Tinker Toys, Lincoln Logs

or collected the rubber-banded packs of baseball cards.

I try to connect to the lives of real people, but all I find

is the detritus of faceless numbers.

In the last booth, I run my finger along the dusty shelf

of a small bookcase in one dark corner of the rented stall

and touch a well-worn elementary reader from 1910. I open

the front cover, and read a name inscribed

in careful cursive, Shelley Jacob Ashton, 1918.

Thumbing through the pages, I notice several

have been folded in a tiny triangle at the top corner;

I know what that means. At last, I am pulled

into another life as I settle

into a blue chintz armchair

and follow the dog-eared trail.

I spend the afternoon

getting to know Shelley Jacob Ashton

as he guides me to his favorite lands away.

Felix P. Sepulveda

The Achilles Heel

His name was Father Mesa, and I compared him to the kind, nurturing priests I saw in movies like Pat O'Brien or Bing Crosby and wondered, at the age of 9, if religion was compatible with reality. He was a good looking man with his olive complexion, black hair, coiffed a la Bobby Darrin for all the good that would do him and deep, brown eyes. I used to think that he would have been very popular with the ladies. He glided in front of the pews from one side to another in his floor length black robe demanding our attention as he explained why we partake of the host. Jesus hung down wearing a loin cloth, the last of his worldly possessions, above dozens of us sitting side by side five pews full. Directly below there were golden candelabra's, a golden chalice and expensive silks covering the elaborate altar. The cool air was mixed with a hint of incense whiffling from the open front doors. On the wall to our right was a molded scene of the first station of the Crucifixion. Where Christ's belief was condemned.

I remember Father Mesa's eyes darting from side to side as he scanned the pews for any violator. I never saw him smile. I often wondered if he was mean because he regretted becoming a priest which confounded me because he was sure going to heaven in return for doing God's work. I thought about my quid pro quo with God.

Even so, I never saw him slap a kid for swallowing to loud as the rumor went. Nor did I see any sadistic tendencies when he carried out a punishment. Although, in 1958 Redlands, a small Southern California town, it was quite ok to swat a child in order to save his soul. My soul was saved once.

Now, I must admit there was an amusing thrill watching

Becky, face flushed, obscuring her freckles, glasses clinging to one ear and her chin as her breath frosted one lens, after she viciously whirled around to glare at Freddy. I struggled to stifle a guffaw as I imagined him staring back, mouth shut tight, eyes wide in bewilderment, but I couldn't tell because I had my nose in the Bible at that moment.

I had shot her in the head with a soda straw spit ball three pews behind. The commotion caused an interruption in the lesson as all eyes, except mine, landed on Freddy I understood that Father Mesa had direct communication with God, but I was still stunned when I heard my name, "Feliz", Felix in Spanish. Immediately, fervently I began, "Our Father who art in heaven"…, but my pleas were in vain. Up by my ear to the front of the altar. I heard Jimmy giggling and made a mental note to sock him.

Being swatted in front of your peers is embarrassing, but what made it excruciating, and I think Father Mesa considered this, is that I couldn't cry in front of the girls. It wasn't just me. No self-respecting boy was going to baby-bawl in front of those funny looking creatures that repelled us while compelling us. So, the five swats hurt, but the pain of holding my tears was worse.

****

When I first saw the scar tissue it was through watery eyes. It looked like a dead earthworm glued down the center of his concaved chest. I turned away and wiped my tears with the back of my hand so my brother wouldn't see. That night I strengthened my agreement with a prayer, a promise, and a pleading.

His name was Manuel and he was two years older than me. He's the one who taught me how to catch a bird with a cardboard box, some twine, a stick and some bread crumbs. It worked too. He taught me how to play baseball, football and basketball by playing with me. I could never win when it was just the two of us. He was humiliated enough. His skinny body was easily tired. I didn't mind losing, and he never gloated in his victories. He was my best friend even after the time he blocked the front door as Mom was swatting my behind with a curtain rod. Me climbing his back trying to get out. He laughing as he gripped the side door jams like Hercules on the columns. Then, after I stopped crying, he apologized and made it up to me with a soda from Elmer's Market.

I was a good boy, Becky notwithstanding, and Jimmy didn't count because he deserved a good sock. I didn't smoke. I couldn't lie because my eyes would dart from side to side when questioned. Shit, I couldn't even curse. Never even tried. And, I would never risk seeing the disappointment in my Dad's eyes if I was ever caught stealing. So, I asked God to give my brother half the strength of my heart. Please God just one more miracle. In return I would devote myself to the church. He could do it too. I would be doing half the work.

***

I continued with the church throughout elementary, junior and senior highs. I made my First Holy Communion and my Confirmation, but had I not made a deal with God I would never have endured the humiliation of completing my Communion.

It was the last Friday practice before our Sunday Ceremony. There were three of us walking behind four girls to the church. The girls chattered, giggled and occasionally turned around to see what we were up to. We talked loudly of snakes and lizards and the he-manly things we would do with them as we walked Orange Street past a florist shop situated in a private home. Bouquets were displayed in the front picture window with a blue curtain hanging behind. We continued past an ice cream parlor where we turned right at the gas station.

Frances was one of the four girls in front of us. She had flowing black hair, brown eyes and a soft, creamy, brown complexion. I loved to watch the sway of her hips so when Robert wanted to stop and buy a soda at the gas station I tried to talk him out of it. I almost had him too cause we were late, but then he made me an offer I couldn't refuse. He offered to buy me one. Not one of the small 8oz bottles, he bought me a big 16 oz., RC Cola.

By the time we got to the church, our sodas were gone. I offered to throw Roberts empty bottle away and scurried to one of the old pepper trees on the side of Saint Mary's to stash the 3 cents apiece treasures for a later time. As I covered them in a hole in the trunk with old bark, I peeked around the tree and debated whether or not I should try to get away with peeing. Then I looked up to the bell tower crowned with the cross and decided not.

Kids were grouped in their respective cliques talking about everything except Communion. There was a sustained rumble with an occasional screech as horseplay and conversations continued. When Father Mesa came out and clapped his hands all that could be heard was shuffling shoes as kids scurried, like panicked roaches, to form two lines. Boys were on one side, the girls were on the other. Father Mesa walked back into the church to the altar and turned around. Then he clapped once again. His lips were tight shut. His eyes were narrowed by the crease of his forehead as we entered the church. We ceremoniously walked in, applied holy water in the sign of the cross and genuflected before sliding into the correct pews. Each of us hoping there were no mistakes.

An hour into the rehearsal and it hurt. I felt like somebody was poking my penis with a needle. I should have peed when I had the chance. There was no way I was going to enrage Father Mesa by stopping his gig so that I could use the restroom. Besides I didn't want the girls to know that I had to pee. The standing and sitting was aggravating my situation. Each time we practiced a prayer I was praying in earnest. Please God make this end. I felt as if the needle had gotten bigger. I dropped and rolled my head and prayed harder. I wanted to squeeze my penis to aid in its battle but I knew that wouldn't look right. Stand, kneel, sit and each time I thought I was going to lose it. I asked God to take just a little of the pain, and when He didn't I remembered He had ignored the pleas of Jesus as part of their deal.

Finally, we were on our knees engaged in our last prayer. Hurry, I thought to myself. I might make it. Then stupid Walter raised his hand to ask a stupid question. As the Nun explained the answer, I mean a deep, philosophical answer, I knelt in agony. I couldn't take it anymore. Ok, I couldn't whip it out and relieve myself so I decided to sneak just a tiny bit as we knelt. The plan was to leak just a little every now and then until I could get out and run home. I knew God would understand, but I knew Father Mesa wouldn't if I got caught. I tried to squirt, but once I relaxed it was like a bursting water main. My urine gushed and try as I may I could not arrest the torrential flow. Everyone was in prayer and quiet reflection. The only sound in the cavernous church was the flow of urine as it hit my coarse, new Levi pants and flowed down my thigh and then out the pant leg. The sound and ammonia smell quickly caught the attention of Jesse who knelt next to me. Despite my look of warning, then pleading, Jesse looked down at the forming puddle, raised his hand and loudly, laughingly told the entire world that I peed my pants. The Nun, perhaps considering Father Mesa's temperament, simply said, "That's ok", and continued with closing the ceremony. I was sure I would be the laughing stock of the school as I ran home when we were released. However, by Holy Communion Sunday everyone was too engrossed with tradition, their families and their new clothes to mention it much. But, I was mortified whenever the incident came up. I never wanted to go back to that church. Again I thought about Jesus suffering for humanity and decided I could face humiliation and half my heart for my brother.

****

In junior high, when I became fully mesmerized, I hated losing my weekends. Saturday and Sunday were the best times to gawk at girls at the Sylvan plunge, or sit next to at the Fox Theatre. And I was going to sit next to one too, but to do that I needed money. And that meant jumping in and out of the Hockridge Florist delivery van when I wasn't in school. So, just as soon as one of his co-workers quit, Manuel got me my first morning paper route. Yes, freedom, but there is a price to pay for freedom.

We would get up at 3:00 AM every morning whether in the freezing rain, the blustering wind, which made it twice as hard to ride your bike, or the piercing, clear cold that frosted our labored breath. We left our well-lit neighborhood and bravely pedaled around a mile and a half down, aptly named, Orange Street. We would ride our bikes through the pitch black darkness that hung over the groves leading to downtown. The dark, coldness on each side camouflaged the occasional leafless, dying tree that I was sure was a monster with extended arms. I absolutely didn't want to see one of those trees reach up and pick its own orange and throw it at me as I saw the apple tree do on "The Wizard of Oz." That was not entertaining. That was terrifying. The Wolfman, Frankenstein and Dracula were popular movies around that time, and I quickly learned all my prayers from catechism, but my brother provided more solace with just his presence.

Once we passed the 5 & 10 Store I felt like we had entered the safety of Emerald City. There was a long, well lit, downhill freebie that we used to coast into the business district. We passed a bowling alley, barber shops, Eddie's

Liquor, Bank of America, and at the main intersection there was a shoe shine/repair shop around the corner from two competing pool parlors sitting side by side. On the adjacent corner, with its name in bright neon lights, the grand, old, La Posada Hotel stood right out of a James Cagney movie. You couldn't miss it if you were a kid because on the roof was a huge ice cream cone sign that invited hungry children, parent in tow, to visit the shop next to the hotel. There we turned left one half block down a scary alley to a building in back of the former police station. It was an old, red brick, livery stable. There was one long row of cubicles on one side. A bike rack on the other. Each station contained a small table with a clip for your "kicks", a complaint about delivery, and a paper tier that looked like a spindly, black sewing machine with a raised arm and a spool of heavy string sitting on its top. Thirty to forty minutes to tie and load our papers and we were out to the surrounding neighborhoods.

Redlands was incorporated in 1888 and has a rich blend of grand old homes, modern, single family homes displaying dichondra yards with automatic sprinklers and small, pristine, wooden houses behind hedges. To avoid receiving a "kick", a good newsboy learned where and when the sprinklers turned on, which customer wanted their paper on the porch and which of the "husbands" preferred to tip toe in, or out as the case may be, through the side door. And, to encourage a big tip on the most important family holiday, he hand delivered the customers Christmas card with his lips shut tight and a twinkle in his eye.

My favorite part of the morning was meeting Manuel at the Oasis Café, next to the shoe shop, after our deliveries. The golden glow emanating from the two big plate glass windows that straddled the single, front door entrance was visible many blocks away. I glided down the morning grey, cold street with anticipation. It was a diner barely encompassing the horseshoe counter in the middle. He always bought me breakfast as we exchanged stories about the morning deliveries. Counter service only, but it was the most delicious eggs over-easy, juicy ham, golden brown potatoes, toast and coffee I ever had each time. I remember once, as my ears began to absorb the warmth of the room, the familiar surrounding chatter and the clatter of silver ware and porcelain, my brother sat beside me laughing. He told me about a dog that attacked him from the back yard of a Ward Cleaver type home. It had a white picket fence in front but no back yard partitions or walls. Manuel said he heard the bark turn to a snarl as the German Shepard bolted from a dog house in the back and was so anxious to get a taste of his leg that it forgot about the swimming pool. My brother made the sound of a splash and a yelping dog and laughed again just before he chomped on his toast. I laughed with him because he was safe, and it was good to see him nourish his body.

****

In my senior year I noticed a caterpillar clinging upside down on a branch next to my bedroom window. I thought it was dead as it didn't move. My curiosity each day allowed me to witness the insect as it changed from an ugly, dangling caterpillar, to a dangling cocoon, to emerge as a magnificent black and gold, adult butterfly. I marveled at the things God could do.

I waited anxiously for a similar metamorphosis to occur for my brother. I grew some and gained muscular weight by the time I went to high school. He did not. Well, he did get taller but his body remained slender and his chest remained that of a little boy. He seemed tired and listless. I knew why, and I knew he was in a downward spiral. I wrestled with the way God was conducting our agreement.

Manuel had graduated and began delivering for Hockridge Florist during the day, and both of us continued to get up every morning at 3:00 AM to toss papers now from our Volkswagen beetles. His was red. Mine was black, and he helped me with the initial down payment. Both Manuel and I had been waking at 3:00 AM every day since 7th grade. I played football and wrestled throughout high school, and the lack of sleep coupled with the physical exertion took a heavy toll on my body. I stretched to a soaring 5' 5". Manuel was a little taller, but he looked weak, and the drugs and alcohol didn't help.

****

I continued to keep my part of the bargain despite my growing concerns. I attended church and confession which was a real problem because when I became a teenager I discovered the reason those funny looking creatures compelled us so. I hated telling Father Mesa what I was thinking when it came to girls. So, I used the generic "I had bad thoughts", phrase. If I had told him the orgiastic scenes that played in my mind, I would have had to bring lunch to complete my penance.

I had thought the change to the caterpillar was something, but what happened to girls was wonderful. God truly is great. I thought the jiggling, growth of their chests was fascinating but always wondered, until I found Playboy, what was under those clingy blouses. Watching a girl in short shorts was more captivating than the beauty of the butterfly, and it caused things to happen to me that I didn't understand. I, actually probably most of us, knew nothing about sexuality.

We did know about the teachings of the Church. We were forbidden to think of girl's bodies or sharing our bodies, yet that's all we thought about. I began to wonder if that was why Father Mesa was so grumpy. My belief in the teachings of the Church was conflicted by the reality that we were all, boys and girls, very interested in sex. I believed them when they told me I was hurting God when I thought of sex outside of marriage. I was told that I would burn in hell if I didn't confess my sins. But what really scared me was the God's truth rumor among us boys. At thirteen I began to shave my right palm every morning in order to hide any hairy evidence of a normal, natural act of adolescence because it was a sin in God's eyes. That was my second strike with the Church.

****

Ten years after my First Communion disaster I walked into St. Mary's and I could sense doubt, like a serpent, coiling around my mind. The soft organ music didn't inspire. I knelt in front of a miniature stadium of red candles and made the sign of the cross. The perpetual sweet aroma of incense was contrasted with the heavy smell of melting candle wax. I picked up one of the long matches and lit it from one of the burning candles. My hand shook uncertainly as I lit a candle for my brother and began to pray. I felt the words burn from my heart, rise in the air and disperse like the smoke of the incense.

Anger overtook me. I was tired of being conflicted. The beauty and passion I had recently discovered with my girlfriend was like nothing in life, or in the church, I had ever experienced. Our love making was not dirty, and I thanked God every day for his gift. I felt no remorse for my actions. Was I not completing the essential physical and spiritual change of life as crucial as caterpillar to butterfly? I saw the incompatibility of religion and reality. And yet, deep inside I knew the miracle of the change in caterpillars and girls was orchestrated by my Creator. I left troubled by the thought of Father Mesa, and how he had to wait until he died to experience, to understand, the essence of life.

After I had gone to the church, I went to the hospital. My parents and I listened to the doctor as he told us of the seriousness and hazard of this operation. He spoke in monotone. I strained to hear some encouragement. But, the operation had to be done. We visited with my brother for a while until it was time to wheel him upstairs to prep him for surgery. As I walked at the foot of the bed down the hallway, I challenged him to a game of pool when he got out. His smile was weak..., sad..., knowing. A cold terror engulfed me. I clasped onto his sheet covered foot and held on until they stopped me at the entrance to the elevator. The doors slowly closed, and we struggled to keep eye contact as the doctors and nurses jockeyed for position. There was a heavy, dull, pain in my chest. This time I didn't try to hide them as tears flowed down my cheeks. I watched him struggle to lift his thin, tired body up on one elbow just to wave good-bye to me. Strike three.

The Gift

Zameer took a break from work and strolled up and down the sidewalk in front of his family's jewelry store on this bright, cold fall morning. Their store was on the historic Old Santa Fe Trail road near the major Alameda thoroughfare. After he checked the dwindling customer traffic, Zameer walked back inside to grab some cleaner and a cloth. When he sidled past the glass case nearest the cash register, he glanced at a photo on the wall. In it, he stood with his three brothers and their much older cousin, Ahmed, their arms draped over each other's shoulders. Ahmed stood in the center of this small group – his usual position among them. Whenever Zameer waffled over making hard decisions, Ahmed would counsel him: "Don't be afraid. Take chances. Live life. No risks make you a smaller man."

That advice now made Zameer bristle; he couldn't admit to his family that he had grown to dislike sales. "What actual impact do I have on people's lives?" he'd chide himself. Had his cousin lived, Zameer knew he'd have some valuable career advice. Zameer hated that Ahmed was gone.

In cousin Ahmed's short 50-year-old life, he had suffered. When Ahmed had first moved to New Mexico in 1986, he'd taken two bullets in the chest from armed robbers. On another occasion, he'd suffered a massive heart attack that doctors couldn't explain. Then, a drunk driver had plowed his car into him head on. And Ahmed had survived it all, with generosity of spirit and heart intact. Zameer once teased him about his ability to cheat death. He joked, "What should I tell the public in my eulogy for you?"

When Zameer wouldn't let up, Ahmed declared, "Say

to them: 'Just this person'." His cousin would never explain what he'd meant. "You'll figure it out," was all he'd say. Zameer thought there would be enough time to discover the answer to Ahmed's infuriating riddle. But his cousin's luck ran out. One morning Ahmed had just stepped outside the front door of his house when an SUV veered off the road, jumped the curb, headed straight for Ahmed and crushed him.

Zameer sighed and looked out the huge storefront window to distract himself. He checked the three long tables outside in their store's tiny courtyard, each of which carried authentic Navajo pottery from local artists. The earthy pinks, oranges, blues and sandstone colors reminded him of the Santa Fe sunsets. Sometimes customers, attracted by the art, would be enticed to enter the store and look around.

A youngish Asian man walked into the courtyard. For a second, Zameer thought the man's manners echoed his cousin's. Zameer watched him carefully pick up and examine some of the smaller vases. Minutes later, the man walked inside the store. He had picked the only small vase with a design that stood out: melted dark coffee-colored horsehairs on an off-white soap stone surface imitated sepia-toned squiggles, like small Sumi-e paint brush dashes.

Zameer walked behind the cash register. The man placed the vase on the counter and then left his denim shopping bag at his feet. Zameer exchanged greetings with the customer, sizing him up. The young man's violet-flecked brown eyes contrasted his tawny skin and dull, chestnut-colored hair.

The man tapped the vase's lip. "How much?"

Zameer placed one hand on the counter, his other palm upturned, gesturing as he spoke. "Twenty-five dollars. Signed on bottom by the Navajo artist himself. A good deal." He watched the man's reaction to the price, trying to gauge what kind of spender he was.

The man said he'd look around the store while he

decided on the vase. He took his time studying all the cased jewelry.

Zameer followed him around to answer any questions, ready to pull out any items to show the customer. But he kept a respectful distance.

Zameer knew he only had precious moments to make his customer trust him. The longer he could get him to stay, the greater the chance he'd buy more than just the vase. Zameer asked him what he was looking for and then pulled out some samples from the cases. He said, "Most people want precious Southwestern stones but don't want to pay the price for them. But there's hardly any real turquoise left in New Mexico. Prices will only go up."

The man's mouth looked like a flat line. Zameer was used to uptight customers. He kept up the spare but easy-going chatter. He wanted the customer to let down his guard. Getting him to chuckle might do the trick.

Zameer cleared his throat. "You know, my cousin, Ahmed, he shaped our family business. Can you believe it, thirty years ago, he had traveled to China with only a thousand dollars in his pocket. He made deals there and came back with merchandise that jump-started our original family business."

When the man barely responded, Zameer blurted out a question that seemed to get most Asian customers to talk. "You Chinese?"

Zameer thought he saw the man frown a bit before he answered. "No. Japanese American."

Zameer continued. "Can you tell what I am? Go on, guess."

"I really can't say."

Zameer, now on the other side of the case, kept pressing him.

His last plea drew the man out. "I don't know. Maybe Iranian? Or, Turkish?"

Zameer smiled and tapped his own chest. "Jordanian," he revealed and waited for the usual polite acknowledgment from the customer.

Zameer pointed to himself and then his customer. "We're the same. Both Asian, right?"

The younger man looked confused and then he chuckled. "That's right. You're absolutely right."

Zameer felt lighter now, like he was wearing a balloon suit filled with helium, making gravity less burdensome. Sometimes the life of a merchant could be lonely. Hustling people into spending their money on expensive jewelry made him feel empty. Making a genuine connection with this customer might be fun. He soon discovered the customer was in town for a historical studies conference and that this was his first visit to Santa Fe.

The young man revealed that his father had been in an internment camp not too far away from Santa Fe during World War II – Camp Amache in Colorado – and then later a U.S. Army facility called Camp Lordsburg in southern New Mexico. "My mother was interned at Manzanar; she was born there."

Zameer had heard about Manzanar. "Where's Amache?"

"In Granada. Southeastern Colorado."

Zameer snapped his fingers. "Yes, I thought I heard of it before. Granada became a boom town on the old Sante Fe trail again after '42," he said. "No wonder, with all that slave labor."

His customer nodded.

Zameer paused, looked into the customer's eyes, and murmured, "So, we are both descendants from the desert."

The young man's eyes widened. Zameer appreciated that his customer had revealed such information to him.

They continued to chat as his customer walked around the store and viewed the other glass cases. Once done, the man strolled back toward the register. He placed his denim shopping bag onto the counter like it was filled with precious cargo. "I also want an estimate on something," he said.

Zameer watched the man pull out of the bag what looked like an old sterling silver jewelry box.

"How much would it cost to affix a turquoise to the lid?"

Zameer glided behind the counter and pulled the filigreed-edged box toward him. "It's a beautiful piece."

The man beamed. "It's my mother's. My father and I thought it would be a nice surprise to add a gem to the lid. Her birthday's coming up."

"Where did your mother get this box?" Zameer continued his admiration. "It is exquisite."

The man shrugged. "I don't know. My mother hasn't told me much about her life before she met my dad. I'm old enough to hear the truth. I'm a historian. And her son, for god sakes." He sighed. "Her elusiveness has been frustrating."

Zameer nodded. He brought out a velvet-lined tray of turquoises. As the two looked at them, the man shifted gears and explained how devoted his parents were to each other.

"What's your mother's name? We could engrave her name in the box."

"Midori. Midori Eriko Morimoto."

The young man took the opportunity to talk about his mother – he went on about her devotion to his father and the family. As he listened to the young man, Zameer completed the invoice for the estimate and set aside the chosen turquoise. The man then looked at the wall clock, and a guttural sound escaped from his throat. "Ah, I've gotta run. I'm going to be late to my conference session. When'll the estimate on the box be ready?"

Zameer said a few hours.

The man nodded. "I'll be back to pick up my vase and get your quote." He handed his credit card over to Zameer to pay for the vase. "I want to take the box to another jewelry store for a second estimate before the end of the day, so I can make a decision by tomorrow morning."

Zameer forced a smile. Now back in his selling mode, he wasn't happy to hear that he had competition. He studied the credit card and made note of his customer's name: Brent Morimoto. He then rang up the vase and handed over the estimate invoice for the box. "See you later, Brent."

The merchant watched his customer turn and dash out of the store. Zameer vowed that Midori would love the beautiful turquoise on her box.

. . .

Sometime later, Zameer approached his brother Thaman, a certified stone-cutter. He was in the back workroom sitting at his work table finishing his cost assessment of the turquoise stone placement on the jewelry box lid. After a quick exchange of words, Zameer wasn't happy.

Thaman grunted. "I don't care. Make sure you underbid so the customer doesn't decide on another jeweler. A slightly flawed stone will still look pretty. Just don't tell him and he'll never know the difference."

Zameer didn't like what his brother had to say. "Ahmed would've never done that."

Thaman, who then removed his jeweler's loupe, glared at his brother. "It's not that under-handed, Zameer." He raised his voice. "Look, Ahmed's gone. And we need the business."

Zameer frowned and walked away. His throat felt tight. He went back to polishing a large glass case filled with some of the most expensive bracelets and earrings in the store, rubbing more vigorously now. Every now and then, he glanced up at the photo of his cousin on the wall, recalling again his words: *"Just this person."*

What did Ahmed mean? Whenever he felt stressed about the business, Zameer's desire to know would come back with a vengeance. If only his cousin had lived, the family would all be better off with him at the helm.

Zameer grabbed a new cleaning cloth and prayed for more customers.

. . .

Later, he took the box from the back workroom and placed it on the counter near the cash register. He took a polishing cloth and lovingly burnished the surface of the jewelry box, taking off all traces of fingerprints and oxidation.

He stiffened as he thought about having to cheat Brent. *Thaman figures we'll never see my customer again.* But to Zameer it wasn't that easy. *That box means something to Brent's family,* he thought. He propped open the lid and started polishing inside the box.

To complete the job, he gently lifted the thick red velvet lining that crackled due to age and made small circular movements with the cloth across the box's smooth bottom. When he got close to one edge, he felt the cloth catch on something. He held the box up closer to his face and saw an etching of some sort. He turned and sidestepped to a nearby table, putting the box underneath a vise-clamp magnifying glass with a high-powered light.

As his eyes adjusted, he saw three words: *Midori Eriko Chesterton.*

Zameer's mind went fuzzy, as if an enormous dandelion in full bloom had burst inside his head, the floating seeds scattering everywhere. He stared at the mother's name. Why would she have that surname etched in her jewelry box? A prickling twinge snaked up his neck. His cheek twitched. *Midori may have kept something like a previous marriage from her past a secret from her son. Brent had said he knew little about her life before she'd met his father.* Zameer's hands curled into tight balls.

The merchant looked up at the wall clock. Even if he

covered over the mother's previous name with the velvet again, the next jeweler who gave an estimate on the box might find the etched name upon inspection and point it out. Maybe the discovery of her engraved name would be a non-issue to Brent, but Zameer felt uneasy nonetheless. He went outside in the cold, to clear his head. The merchant next door had a small Koi pond in his courtyard, which was clear of customers. Zameer stopped there and stared at the water. *Why couldn't Ahmed be here to ease the problems of this business?* Ahmed knew how to run a profitable business but also make real connections with customers.

Zameer watched the fish for a while, trying to figure out what to do. What did Ahmed mean when he'd told him, "Just this person"? Zameer repeated the phrase over-and-over in his mind. His head started to hurt.

He glared at his own reflection in the water and said aloud, "It makes no sense – 'Just this person . . . . Just this person . . . *Just . . . this . . . person.*'"

The last time he repeated the phrase, Zameer's eyes widened. He saw his reflection mingle with the gliding Koi, their jeweled bodies swirling in harmony. He saw how the blue sky and fluffy clouds could be seen in the water's surface. Then, as he heard a flock of birds fly overhead, he saw the last remnants of their formation glide over the water's surface. He now saw the beauty of it all.

His cousin shouted from his grave. Zameer felt like all the pores on his face had opened.

He realized what "Just this person" could mean. "I am *just this person,*" he said. His cousin had wanted him to see that a person not only enters the world alone, he leaves the world alone. Loving himself would help him become unstuck in his life and to let go of false expectations. "I'm who I am," he thought. "Not who I or anyone else thinks I should be." This process of choosing how to think for himself began now.

Ahmed's insight was his gift to Zameer.

He remembered the last time the generous Ahmed cooked for the entire family. "Come and eat. Be happy," Ahmed exclaimed, stretching out his arms as if he wanted to encircle the entire clan as they gathered around the dining room table to sample his delicious tender lamb and other savory dishes.

Only a few days after Ahmed's last supper with the family, he was dead. Run over by a truck in front of his house. Just like that. But he had lived when he was alive. Eyes wide open. Reveling in his own joy and sharing his good fortune with others. He always chose to help others, whether they were family or not.

As Zameer returned to the store, he reflected that Ahmed's death had happened almost two years ago, now. Ahmed was gone. Zameer knew he would still mourn the loss of this man and his spirit for some time to come. But maybe the anger and sadness of wanting him back would one day pass.

Zameer finished polishing the lid on the sterling silver jewelry box, wiping his remaining fingerprints off its surface.

. . .

When Brent returned to the store, Zameer watched how he strode inside. Brent's cheeks were ruddy from the cold, his eyes bright with anticipation.

Zameer waited for him to reach the counter. With a flourish, he brought out the jewelry box from under the counter near the register and placed it before Brent. As he looked at the now cheery young man, his knees weakened a bit.

"I hope your quote's within my price range," Brent said, rubbing his palms together.

Zameer took a deep breath. As he straightened his back, he felt the vertebrae in his spine make tiny popping sounds of protest. "I'm afraid it's probably more expensive than you want." He'd decided not to cheat Brent even at the expense of the business. He also decided not to hide his mysterious discovery from him. Zameer would soon find out if Brent knew the story behind the engraving. He also hoped the young man would accept it if his mother still refused to reveal her past.

Ahmed's message to wake up also helped Zameer understand that compassion for others would come when he placed his own emotional suffering in perspective. *I am not the sun. I am a planet -- among other planets.* Zameer hoped to share the effects of Ahmed's gift with Brent. "Before I give you the estimate...," Zameer swiveled around and took down the family photo from the wall. "There's something I want to share with you." The merchant handed the picture over to Brent.

Zameer smiled. Sharing with Brent what he'd learned might help fortify Brent no matter what he knew or didn't know or wanted to know. Zameer felt his throat open and his voice emerge: "I want to tell you more about my cousin Ahmed. How he died."

He then leaned closer to the photograph. "And lived."

David Stone

Those Who Sort Their Pain

We often sympathize
with those enduring
the weight of a single
suffering.

We sometimes empathize
with memories
from the pain of our
past.

But what of those
who daily
must sort their
pains?

skin from muscle
organ from bone
joint from tendon

ache,
throb,
cramp

tingling,
radiating,
piercing

physical from phantom

If only they could simply
wash, dry, fold,
and put away
refreshed.

David Stone

Feeling a Fault

My fingernail splits

past the free rim

beyond the quick

deeper than a clip

could trim my plate,

a fault farther than a file

could smooth with grit.

I'm definitely aging

brittle keratin,

feeling fretted like

a shaken Californian,

certain I'm doomed

for perennial fissure.

My Mother Said I Hope

you marry a woman who tells you

how worthless you are.

your wife only buys

Christmas presents for herself.

you raise at least two

children who fight all day.

your doctor prescribes medicine

that doesn't touch your pain.

you never live

in a house of your own.

your children tell you exactly

how you raised them wrong.

 you have to ask

your children for a loan.

Yes, Mother said I hope

you know the blessing

every time I say a curse.

David Stone

Celebrating the New Year

Dancing long past the last day's dusk,

I spin my daughter in the West.

Cheering the year's first minute in the East,

I count nine as twelve because she's eight.

Ignoring the rules, we step out of time,

tracking not a circle on the Earth,

or a cycle through the air,

but the joy of being

in each other's eyes.

Judith Turian

How This Jewish American Princess Became Catholic

Leading a spiritual life requires the willingness to be surprised by God. My spiritual path has been filled with surprises, and I view any degree of willingness I've had as a gift from God. Other than the basics of the genetic loading with which I entered the world and the warring influences of my critical mother and unconditionally loving father who was incapable of providing any useful criticism, it is my lifelong spiritual journey that has made me who I am today.

I had my first spiritual experience when I was five years old. To this day, I don't know if it was a dream, a daydream or a visitation. I saw myself with my curly hair bathed in sunlight, making the reddish highlights sparkle and shine. I was sitting on a swing wrapped in thick colorful ribbons, and there was a dazzling rainbow in the sky above. While I was swinging, an angel appeared. I can't describe the angel. I can't even say whether my angel was a man or a woman. I don't think I saw this angelic presence so much as I knew it was there, telling me that I was here for something special.

I don't know what that meant specifically. It has meant different things for me at different times throughout my life. I would have the greatest romance ever. I would become a famous speaker and lecturer and travel around the world to the applause of adoring and thankful audiences. Since I found God and a spiritual way of life, my ambition has been to be the best me I can be, to do God's work, to love and serve others and most importantly, to be my daughter Shaina's mom.

What I know is that the visitation and the message helped me through the hardest and blackest times in my life--losing my first love, drowning in addiction, being passed over for a longed for promotion. Because of the belief that I was here for something special, I always had hope and faith that things, whatever things were, would turn out.

Every summer from the year I turned six until I was 14, I was sent away for eight weeks of all girls' camp in the magnificent Adirondack Mountains. I loved it. The Philadelphia contingent of campers left behind their waving parents and climbed onto a bus headed for Grand Central Station in New York. There we met up with the New Jersey and New York girls, and we boarded the B&O (Baltimore and Ohio) overnight train bound for Saranac Lake, New York. We had bunk beds on the sleeper cars, and for me, it was magical, kind of like the train to Hogwarts that the witches and wizards took back to school every year. And my feelings were much the same as Harry Potter's—I got to escape from home and be free. I got to belong to something larger: the bunk, the green team and color war, the campfires, the camp songs and Camp Navarac itself. And it was here that my religious training began and took root.

The camp was for Jewish girls, and we had services in the big tent every Saturday morning. Each week, several bunks were chosen to put on the service. I learned to love the prayers and beautiful minor key hymns chanted or sung in Hebrew: the Sh'ma, the Kodosh. The prayer books at camp and in synagogue printed the words in Hebrew on one page and the transliteration, or phonetic spelling, on the opposite page, so that we could learn to say the words or sing the prayers.

Halfway through the summer was parents' weekend when all the parents would come to visit, usually laden with candy and gifts. We all wanted the Sugar Daddies and Jujubes and Three Musketeers and licorice, but not so much the parents. The most magical part of parents' weekend for me, and I think for everyone, was the Saturday morning service which, for that occasion, was led by the camp owner, Aunt Sarah Blum. The highlight of the service was Aunt Sarah's reading of *The Little Engine That Could*. There was never a dry eye in the tent by the end of the reading, and I am convinced that any girl who ever went to Camp Navarac was changed forever by that story. I know that I was. The angel let me know that I had a mission or a purpose that was special, and the Little Engine let me know that if I persevered, just kept saying, "I think I can", I could get to the top of the mountain, and then I could breathe a sigh of relief and joyfully say, "I knew I could. I knew I could. I knew I could."

Camp Navarac was located on the shores of Saranac Lake and mostly hidden in the dense woods of the majestic Adirondack Mountains. The breathtaking beauty and deep peace of this setting formed the backdrop of my camp spiritual experience. The smell of the pine needles soft underfoot, the surrounding comfort of the forest paths, the joy and freedom I experienced on the lake, canoeing and sailing and aquaplaning and swimming, the soft muted sound of the rain falling in the woods are still with me after all these years. Scripture says that the sound of God is in the gentle breeze and the still small voice within. To me, the mountains, woods or even the leaves blowing in the trees outside my patio door today all carry the sound of the Holy Spirit that I learned, without knowing it was what I was learning, when I was just a girl at camp.

There was no talk of God or religion or spirituality at home. The closest thing to religious philosophy that I encountered was my father's absolute belief in "Que sera sera," meaning "Whatever will be will be." And I do think he genuinely had an attitude of surrender to the what is, a faith that all will work out, a sense (though never stated) of God's will.

My parents' version of Jewish tradition was limited to attendance at synagogue for High Holiday services. We celebrated Rosh Hashanah (Jewish New Year) with a big, delicious family meal of roast beef, creamed spinach, mashed potatoes and Challah bread. Come to think of it, the central organizing principle of my secular Jewish family life had to do with food—lox and bagel on Sunday mornings, chopped liver and crackers while waiting for any holiday meal to be served, deli sandwiches or Mandarin American Chinese for Thursday night maid's night off and dairy, dairy, dairy—sour cream and fruit in the summer, cream cheese and jelly sandwiches or ice cream anytime. Any excuse for a big meal would do. This included Friday night dinner when my sister and brother-in-law routinely visited or any holiday that Hallmark cards was celebrating regardless of its religious or ethnic origin.

The other major High Holiday was Yom Kippur, the Jewish Day of Atonement. The Indian summer weather in late September or early October inevitably made us miserable as we dressed up in our newest winter woolen outfits to go to temple. I loved the Kol Nidre service with its beautiful and sad music and prayers. My parents' experience, however, was expressed best by their unspoken remarks. "How soon can we leave synagogue without being noticed?" or "How fast can we stop fasting?"

Our upper middle class suburban Jewish culture required us to belong to the Jewish country club where parents played golf and spent money on lavish Bar and Bat Mitzvahs, Sweet 16 parties and weddings. During Christmas vacation, my Jewish family, along with many others took off for Miami to stay at one of the fancy hotels such as the Fountainbleu, Eden Roc or Boca Raton Resort where they played more golf, ate more food, and dressed up in formal clothes for the evening entertainment. This routine was repeated in the summer with the location changed to the Catskill Mountain resorts—The Concord, Grossinger's or Brown's Hotel. Of course, neither the food nor the parties nor the resort vacations helped me get any closer to religion, spirituality or relationship with Abba,

Father, God.

Jewish history communicated at home consisted of the usual awareness of prejudice and struggle by the chosen people throughout time with the most horrendous example, of course, being the Holocaust. Nevertheless, Mom and Dad filled their parental religious responsibilities by sending me to Sunday School at Main Line Reform Synagogue starting in 1st grade and continuing until 10th grade when I was confirmed on Shavuot, a Jewish holiday which followed about the same amount of time after Passover as the Pentecost follows Easter. Since Jewish girls, at that time, were rarely Bat Mitzvahed, Confirmation was the consolation prize. And, of course, there was a party with lots of food and presents. So, why not?

All my friends went to Sunday school, but, as far as I know, I was the only one who absolutely loved going. Maybe no one talked about liking it because it wasn't cool; I don't know. But I did. We had two areas of study—one was Jewish history as presented in the Torah (first five books of the Bible) and the rest of scripture (known in the Christian world as the Old Testament). The other was modern Hebrew. We were also required to attend Saturday morning services several times each year.

When I was 8 or 9 years old, Edwina was our live-in maid. She was, in some ways, a surrogate mother, a stand-in caregiver, a nanny (though my mother would never have elevated her, in her mind or estimation, to the position of nanny). Edwina was, to my mother's way of thinking, the 'schwarza' (Yiddish for Negro). She took care of me, made the rules, kept me clean and fed. But most important of all, she inadvertently introduced me to Jesus. Every Easter season, I was glued to the TV, watching the traditional movies, "*The Robe*" and "*Barrabas*." Edwina must have observed my fascination with Jesus, and she informed me that the sun always disappeared behind the clouds between 1 and 3 on

Good Friday because that's when Jesus was crucified. This made a huge impression on me.

Somehow, during that time, I had taken to gasping if I was startled or frightened, crossing myself and saying, "Jesus, Joseph, and Mary." I don't know where I learned this. My friends and acquaintances were all Jewish. I don't remember ever knowing, let alone being friends with, anyone Catholic, or even Christian. Maybe I saw this in school or on TV. I don't know, but I began praying to God to forgive me if Jesus was really his son, because how could I know this coming from a Jewish family?

By 10th grade, when I was in Confirmation class with Rabbi Gordon, I had somehow gotten enough knowledge of scripture to ask the Rabbi how he knew that Jesus wasn't the Son of God or that the devil wasn't "Lucifer, Daystar, son of the morning." He didn't answer, or maybe he gave some wholly unsatisfactory answer. During Hanukkah when I was in 11th grade, I was furious with my parents because they couldn't wait to eat while I lit the candles on the menorah and said the prayer. It was beside the point that we had never lit Hanukkah candles before, at least not before the meal. Sometimes they were lit on the first night so my parents had a reason to give a present. Our family was amazingly generous when it came to gift giving. I was so mad about the Hanukkah candles and prayer snub that I went on strike from our annual Hanukkah bush (Christmas tree) decorating. I sat on the stairs sulking while the rest of the family merrily strung the multi-colored lights, hung the ornaments and finished the job, delicately draping the tinsel and placing Santa at the top to oversee the holiday goings on. No one took notice of my misery, and by Christmas morning, I had given up the cause in favor of the thrill, even at the advanced age of 16, of opening my Christmas presents.

That same year, I went to Europe with my parents, and

I fell in love with Gothic cathedrals, medieval religious art, and Renaissance sculpture. I was particularly awestruck by images of the Madonna and Child, the love of the mother for the infant and child and her sorrow at his death. I didn't really know much about the scriptural meaning of these portrayals, but somehow they resonated with truth and a holiness that I didn't understand. I was also fascinated by priests and nuns who were everywhere in the churches, museums, and the streets of Rome and Florence. This attraction to Christian religious art continued through the years. When I was at the University of Wisconsin studying Russian History, I fell in love with the ancient Orthodox icons and the chanting of the ancient Church Slavonic monks. In my 20's in New York, I found The Cloisters, a reconstruction of medieval monasteries and abbeys, a peaceful and enchanting place to visit.

I kept trying to establish Jewish faith and connection, but I kept running into weird obstacles. First, there was the rabbi in my confirmation class who didn't take my questions seriously. Then there was the whole college and sorority experience. At University of Wisconsin, I kept trying to rush the Jewish sororities, but they apparently were not interested in rushing me. I was turned down at the Jewish sororities during my freshman and sophomore years while I was offered invitations to join two of the Christian sororities. I kept holding out for an invitation to join a Jewish sorority since I was a Jewish girl. But when I transferred to the University of Pennsylvania for my junior year, history repeated itself, so I finally surrendered and pledged Kappa Delta with the Christian girls. One of my sorority sisters grew up in the soybean fields of Delaware. She had never met a Jewish person before, and she gasped with surprise that I didn't have horns—SERIOUSLY! Many of the girls I met thought that John Milton's *Paradise Lost*, required English lit reading telling the story of Satan and the fall of the rebellious angels, was as authentically scriptural as the creation story or the crucifixion. This general lack of knowledge and understanding was demonstrated by the national sorority representatives who supported recruitment of Jewish girls "as long as they were also Christian!" WHAT? My religious education was definitely limited, but even I knew more or better than some of the ignorant people, girls and adults, that I met in college.

I applied to 14 graduate programs throughout the country after I decided to become a

psychologist. My undergraduate grades weren't great since I was so busy partying that I didn't give much time to studying. Since my bachelor's degree was in Russian History, not psychology, my Graduate Record Exam scores in psychology were in the toilet. I wasn't sure I'd be accepted to any of the schools to which I applied, but in the end, I received acceptance letters at two schools. Wouldn't you know it? Both were Catholic universities run by the Vincentian order of priests!

After I graduated with my doctorate in psychology in 1978, I had to go to work. I had four job offers but lost them all before I started, due to cut backs in funds and hiring freezes. So I joined the US Navy. Six weeks later, I was assigned to take a two week class on the Alcoholic Rehabilitation Service where I was to learn to recognize and refer alcoholics for treatment. However, by the end of the first week of class, I was ordered to stay as a patient in treatment for my own alcoholism. The first thing I heard in treatment was that I had to find a "God of your own understanding" who could help me recover. There was a gorgeous Navy chaplain on staff who was a Catholic priest. Fr. Anton was bright and funny, and I asked him to find a rabbi to talk to me, someone who was similar to him in personality and approach. He knew "just the right guy", and he said he would contact him for me. But "just the right guy" was out of town for an extended period, so the rabbi he found was an old man who thought it wasn't possible for a nice Jewish girl to be alcoholic. This was not going any better than my experience with the rabbi who couldn't answer my questions.

While I was still in treatment, I fell for Huggie who was a fellow patient. We got an apartment together after treatment, and I followed him everywhere.

For Christmas, he gave me a beautiful silver cross. I asked him why he would give a Jewish girl a cross, and he looked at me with surprise and asked, "Why? Don't Jewish girls wear crosses?" I loved that cross and wore it always. Two months later, I asked Fr. Anton to introduce me to the Catholic faith.

I had been attracted to the ritual and tradition of Catholicism ever since my trip to Europe and my study of medieval and Renaissance history in college. It seemed to me to be the first formal Christian religion after Christ and therefore the most authentic. I had some rudimentary understanding that the Catholic mass was based on the Passover ritual and that there were theological connections between Judaism and Catholicism. This gave me some comfort.

Fr. Anton understood the impulsivity of alcoholics and the enticement of strong feelings associated with potentially false spiritual experiences. When he accepted me as a student of the Catholic faith and potential convert, he told me that he would not agree to baptize me as a Catholic unless he believed that I was mature enough in my understanding of the faith and its requirements and that I was not doing this on a whim or because I was hooked on a religious high. At the same time, my AA sponsor wanted to be sure that I was not running away from my past or making a radical decision for the wrong reasons. While I was studying to be Catholic, she asked me to read books about Judaism, metaphysical Christianity (which was studied in the early days of AA before the fellowship had a name and it's own program), and the Big Book which is basic text of Alcoholics Anonymous. She also wanted me to be sure that I wasn't becoming Catholic just because I was wildly enamored with Fr. Anton—remember, he was single (sort of) and gorgeous.

As it turned out (and in my opinion, this was no doubt God's plan), Fr. Anton got orders and transferred for duty in England before he was willing to baptize me. Fr. Tom took his place, and I was definitely NOT in love with him. I really had to decide whether it was Anton or the faith that attracted me. It took another three painful months to decide that I wanted more than anything to become Catholic. On the eve of my first sober AA birthday, I received the sacraments of Baptism, First Holy Communion and Confirmation. This Jewish American Princess was now Catholic, washed clean as snow by the waters of baptism, enveloped in the love of Christ, infused with the Holy Spirit and definitely immersed in a deep and abiding spiritual experience.

Kaleidoscope

(Inspired by a picture of synchronized swimmers)

A mixture of
Art and Math
Along the stream of life.

Teamwork
Teeming, with colors
Orange and blues,
Brilliant hues.

Is it triangles or squares?
A moment in time
Sublime.

Thomas J. Vaden

My First Elephant

In the summer of 1969, I went on an Air Force sponsored retreat to the remote village of Chiang Mai in Northern Thailand where elephants are used to stack and haul massive teakwood logs harvested from the surrounding forests. From these logs, local artisans hewed and hand carved mammoth elephant sculptures and figurines, some larger than real life. After three days of intensive bargaining, I purchased my very first teakwood Asian elephant; a beautiful 30 inch tall, 60 pound specimen with one leg perched atop the belly of a struggling mongoose.

In September, I received an "early out" from U-Tapao AB, Thailand to start graduate studies in mathematics at the University of Missouri. I cleaned out my locker and abandoned my musty military uniforms and civilian clothing on the barracks floor. The Air Force shipped my elephant home free. However, they would not ship my clothes, as the elephant had already exceeded the shipping weight allowance for Air Force personnel on remote tours.

We flew in a cargo plane to Travis AFB in Northern California. We were, in fact, treated like cargo, loosely anchored to the walls in web slings for the duration of the excruciatingly long 18 hour trip. At Travis AFB, I received my discharge papers, deposited my last military uniform on the floor of the dorm and departed with only the clothes I wore on my back. My treasured elephant preceded me to the University of Missouri at Columbia, as did my wife. I had only 10 days to get there and start my classes.

I had to drive the old VW from California to Missouri. On the way, I stopped in Reno and played the slots. I had a few dollars with me when I started gambling and walked out of the Casino with more than $300. In Northern Thailand, the Asian elephant is a symbol of prosperity, good fortune, longevity and wisdom. Thank God I bought the elephant!

I still have my very first elephant after 46 years.

Thomas J. Vaden

Santa Ana Winds

(An unanswered letter to Santa Ana)

How nice thou art to blow away the leaves from my yard and donate them to my neighbors. How mean thou art to knock down my plants that gave me so much pleasure, my treasures.

Why are you so controlling, easily getting my gander? Why are you so irritating, inflicting thoughts that are unfamiliar to my psychic?

Why not be gentle? We would appreciate you more! I do not even want to socialize with you. I'd rather stay in the house, sheltered!

Thomas J. Vaden

Our Neighborhood

My wife, Delia, and I have lived in Hillcrest for 12 years. The neighborhood is somewhat unique for Riverside: a hidden treasure with custom homes on one acre plots. A semi-rural atmosphere prevails, yet we are only one mile from the Mission Grove complex of shopping conveniences that includes a movie theatre, Ralphs and Sprouts grocery stores, K-Mart, CVS Pharmacy, Chipotles, Chiles and LA Fitness. From Alessandro, only two entrances wind into the neighborhood (Overlook and Cannon).

People coming into the neighborhood occasionally get lost. The streets twist around in circular and S-shaped patterns, often changing names as they change directions. Just the other day, a UCR professor visiting a friend accidently turned into our driveway. He was driving in circles for the longest time because he could not figure how to find Alessandro to get back home. I had him follow me out of the subdivision so he could be on his way.

Our neighborhood is unusually quiet, with only the infrequent throbbing of a police helicopter flying overhead, or a cargo aircraft from March Air Reserve Base. The muffled sounds of distant DJ music from a birthday celebration glide up and over the hills. In other neighborhoods, the sounds would rock the walls. Walking the dog around the neighborhood is a daily exercise that allows us to chat with our neighbors.

Our home is perched high on a hill overlooking almost all of Riverside. Every evening, during the first year in our new neighborhood, we would drag our lawn chairs to the driveway to watch the sunset paint a living canvas of clouds, our minds awestruck by an ever-drifting pallet of deep red, yellow, and orange hues interspersed with lighter shades of magenta, cyan, and grey. We had moved from the Wood Streets area of Riverside where there were few opportunities to view the sunsets.

Our home is like an oasis in the center of a sprawling city. Huge well-trimmed Mexican Fan Palms are scattered around the acreage. Our driveway entrance heads up a steep slope with rock gardens located to the left and right. To the west is a small orchard with grapefruit and orange trees. To the east, we created a quiet picnic area surrounded by lush, green gardens. Under large Ficus trees shaped like upside down umbrellas, we built a stamped concrete walkway and an open patio area. We brought in a large mosaic concrete table centered on a huge pedestal and surrounded by four mosaic benches with seating for twelve people. The gardens rise upwards to the lower tree branches providing a peaceful private area to rest and read. We carted in a three foot statue of St. Francis of Assisi to overlook our retreat filled with the sounds of hummingbirds and doves. St. Francis reminds us that we need to contemplate on not what we possess but rather on that which nature bestows upon us.

At night, floodlights illuminate a large antique brass elephant that I purchased in New York years ago. The elephant is very heavy and required two strong men to propel him up our steep driveway on a furniture cart. The statuesque figurine stands five feet tall on his privileged spot on the southeast corner of our property standing guard over the neighborhood. If you have the opportunity to visit our neighborhood, look for the elephant on the hill on Golden Vale Drive.

My Secret Garden

There are times in my life when I want to be left alone. The hustle and bustle of life can be overwhelming. Some days the phone never stops ringing. When this happens, I turn to my serene garden in the Hillcrest area of Riverside. Here, is a distinct connection of being one with nature and the earth.

My garden is a place where family and friends gather. Not too long ago, my husband Tom and I hosted a wedding reception for our daughter Natalie and her husband Rick. I can still see them smiling from ear to ear. It was a joyous time. But today, I want it to be my very own sanctuary.

I have a special area within my garden for meditating. This area sits high on a hill, and only takes up 200 square feet of the acre lot. My feet pulsate as they touch the millions of small pebble-like rocks adorning the ground. Early morning and late evening, it is very cool, putting me in a relaxing mood. Once there, I feel the tension leaving my body, letting me be in the moment.

While I'm sitting on a salmon colored elephant bench surrounded by two Texas Ranger purple bushes and an orange lantana overlooking the neighborhood, I can see a bright red carpet of bougainvilleas for miles and miles, as if setting the hills ablaze with their color and beauty. Here, I feel far removed from everyday stress.

The wind picks up the pungent scents of rosemary, oregano and lavender from the nearby garden, invigorating my sense of smell. The waters from the adjacent elephant shaped fountain, clear my mind and I feel at peace, listening to the soothing gurgling of the water. It seems like only yesterday, I planted bulbs of the amaryllis, now brilliant with red and yellow hues, so beautiful they take my breath away.

Eighteen rose bushes, ranging in color from white, red, pink, orange and golden yellow, are highlighted by the sunlight. They fill the air with sweet aromas. It puts me in a spiritual mood; this is where I kiss the hand of God, thanking him for the various blessings in my life. I am thankful for family, friends, and good health. The glorious sun reflects rays of light from every angle. The grass smells crisp and clean; soon, the cottontails will come to feast on it.

Strolling through the orchard, I smell the rich aroma of citrus blossoms and pick a juicy ripe tangerine. It makes me think of adding tangerine slices to the salad that I will have for dinner.

By retreating to my garden, as I have done, it is no wonder that I feel more alive and rejuvenated. Nothing can compare to spending time with nature and being alone with my thoughts. The only sounds I hear are those of birds chirping, squirrels chasing each other, and an occasional coyote howling at night. It brings true perspective and balance into my life. I am grateful to have such a wonderful place.

This is my garden, my sanctuary, my peace.

Gudelia Vaden

One Sock Up! One Sock Down!

Sitting at the Starbucks' coffee shop at the Galleria in Riverside, CA, my friend Muriel and I are talking about shoes. She rips open her bag with the enthusiasm of a child on Christmas day to show me her new pair of black Nike tennis shoes. Looking around at the busy mall, I noticed the kaleidoscope of colorful shoes as people stroll by. I look down and notice my old New Balance tennis shoes with a fallen sock.

My mind drifts back 65 years to a peaceful time in 1949 during the Truman era, when I lived with my mother and father and six siblings. I was very close to my two sisters, Socorro and Elisa. Socorro was eight and Elisa was three. I was five years old.

My sisters and I loved to play games of all sorts. We would play house on occasion and bring out our dolls and sometimes we would play hopscotch. Many times we would make mud pies in our backyard. But this particular morning, Elisa wanted to play a game called One Sock Up and One Sock Down, a game not unlike Simon Says, but with an odd emphasis on our socks. Elisa would establish the role of Sock Simon and call out, "One sock up!" and we would all inclusively pull up one of our socks. "One sock down!" Elisa cried again, and we all pulled a sock down and so on and so forth. This nonsense could continue for up to 15 minutes or so, but today my father entered the room and interrupted us. He gave us a quick once over, and decided we all had to go to town today.

We all gathered up into his old Ford pickup truck and traveled

10 miles into town. In those days Merced in the San Joaquin Valley had quite a large selection of specialty shoe stores. My parents had a favorite shop for buying our clothes and shoes and that was Montgomery Ward.

At the store, the aroma of fresh leather permeates our senses. It is almost overwhelming. A clerk walks over to us, we point at what we want, and the clerk disappears to only return again with a shoebox under each arm. Elisa and I can barely contain ourselves as it is our turn to get new shoes. We choose Buster Brown high top oxfords in white. As the clerk begins to try them on us, I see the logo of Buster Brown and his dog, Tige inside our Buster Brown shoes. To our delight, the shoes fit like a glove. Father says, "Pretty as a picture!" and we are allowed to wear them out of the store .We cannot wait to get home and show our mother our new pair of shoes.

Father decides he does not have too many pictures of his daughters, so he takes us to a photographer to have our picture taken.

A week later, father drives into town to retrieve the picture. Elisa, Socorro and I laugh as we realized we still had our white cotton socks trimmed with matching lace in the same position as when we were playing our game! One Sock up! One Sock Down!

Frances J. Vasquez

Angelitos Negros

Still wide awake at 10 p.m. one Friday night, I
scrolled the offerings on the cable television guide when I was
pleasantly surprised to see and hear a beautiful Black woman
perform a hauntingly familiar tune in Spanish. On piano. And,
on a regular public television station, not Spanish-language
Univision. Fascinated with the stunning performance, I
hurried to click the select button on the remote control for a
full view of the program. *Oh, my God*, I thought. *She's singing
"Angelitos Negros!"* It was the first time I had seen this old
melancholy song performed on public television. The song
title translates in English to "Little Black Angels." The artist
was crooning a memorable song from my childhood made
famous by Pedro Infante, a legendary Mexican movie star who
was also a popular recording artist. I recalled it was the theme
song from a 1950s dramatic Mexican film by the same name.
It was inspired by a by Venezuelan poet Andrés Eloy Blanco,
"Píntame Angelitos Negros." He wrote the poignant poem in
1946 to decry the lack of paintings depicting Black angels
in South American church artworks. His emotive poem is
considered a hymn, a cry against racial discrimination.

Nostalgic thoughts flooded through me. My senses
went on a tail-spin. It brought me to tears. *Who is she?* I thought.
The songstress looked familiar, but I couldn't recognize her. *Is
this a new retro-rendition of "Angelitos Negros?"* I noticed that
the vocalist was wearing her hair in an Afro, reminiscent of
the 1970s. She and the other two Black male musicians were
dressed in colorful vintage styles from the 1970s era. I was
mesmerized by the soulful melody and sad, evocative lyrics.
Mournfully, the vocalist sang:

"aunque la virgen sea blanca
píntame angelitos negros
que tambien van al cielo
todos los angelitos buenos..."

Roberta's voice lamented: "Although the virgin is white, paint me little Black angels. All good Black angels also go to Heaven." The question Blanco provoked with his poem was why weren't Black angels portrayed in church paintings? It was an ode of protest. My curiosity was piqued. I had to know who this artist was. When the performance ended, I quickly Google-searched my *Smart Phone* to learn that the vocalist/pianist was Roberta Flack. Soul Diva Roberta Flack! The song was from her debut album, "First Take" released in 1969. In this intimate, throw-back 1970s studio performance, the skillful television camera angles captured the soul, the pathos of Blanco's poem: a hymn against racial discrimination. In Roberta Flack's beautiful lyrical voice, I heard her sorrow and angst. The melancholy rhythm of the bass guitar player moved me. The anguish in the drummer's face was apparent. He deftly paced the slow syncopated beat. Together, Roberta Flack and the band performed with appropriate lament.

Hearing and seeing the "Angelitos Negros" music performance sparked within me wistful reflections of my childhood growing up in Highgrove, California. The intense film had an enduring impact. It influenced my world view about race relations and racial discrimination. As I reminisced about "Angelitos Negros," my thoughts drifted back to "el Teatro Azteca" on Mt. Vernon Avenue in San Bernardino where in the mid-1950s I first saw Pedro Infante sing this unforgettable tune in the classic Mexican drama.

I cut my front teeth watching Mexican movies at el Teatro Azteca during the golden age of Mexican cinema. I was fortunate to accompany my mother on occasional movie Sundays. Sooner, but mostly later, the most popular Spanish-language films came to San Bernardino. I have fantastic memories of Mexican cinema depicted on the silver screen: hilarious comedies with Cantínflas and Tin Tan. Lively musicals, like "Allá en el Rancho Grande;" and, intense dramas like "Salón Mexico" and of course, "Angelitos Negros."

Pedro Infante, México's Clark Gable, was my favorite movie idol. He was lovable and handsome with big smoldering dark eyes. He sang popular Mexican tunes like no other: *boleros, rancheras, mambos*. His characters, his songs spoke to me. In my youthful estimation, Pedro could do no wrong – even when he portrayed a notorious "boracho," a drunkard on screen. Pedro, the protagonist in the riveting Mexican film, "Angelitos Negros" helped instill my values of racial diversity and tolerance. I learned as a child to abhor the injustice of racism. The story mattered. It was persuasive. While Pedro's film character depicted the meaning of genuine fatherly love, the film also showed the iniquities of racism. I despised his blond, racist filmic wife for rejecting her own child, just because her daughter was a "negrita." *How terrible! Poor baby. Bad mother. Good father...* those were my thoughts as a eight/nine year old girl viewing the film for the first time. I adored the filmic Pedro for loving his daughter unconditionally.

I remembered a critical scene in the movie that

featured the little Black child sitting on the kitchen floor dusting herself with white flour. When Pedro saw her, he intuitively understood his daughter's fears and insecurities. He ran to her. She somberly asked her father why her mother didn't love her. *¿Porqué mi mamá no me quiere?* She lamented sadly, "Yo la quiero tanto." Pedro tenderly assured his angelic daughter that she is loved and beautiful just the way she is. He gently lifted her off the floor and set her on top of the piano. He lovingly sang to her the "Angelitos Negros" song. Oh, the unrepressed tears flowed at el Teatro Azteca. At a young age, I was forever hooked on the amazing power of film - especially Mexican cinema (which typically eschews the conventional Hollywood happy ending).

My grandmother lived in Providencia, a small dusty village amid the fertile Yaqui Valley within the arid Sonora Desert in México. A tall battery-operated console radio was the focal point in *la sala* of her adobe home. It was her main connection to the rest of the world, and sporadic source of entertainment. Nana's radio was one of only two in the entire village. It didn't always work - poor reception or a dead battery. No one in the village had televisions nor telephones in the mid-1950s. Therefore, the oral tradition of storytelling was our family's favored pastime, especially in the evenings before bedtime. My mother was a wonderful story teller. She was animated and excelled in recounting vivid *cuentos y chistes* - stories and jokes. Mamá captivated us with scary tales of demons and monsters. Our favorites were mythical ghost stories of *La Llorona* and *El Cucúy*. Mamá made us giggle and laugh out loud with funny, light-hearted stories and jokes. She was especially adept at imitating one-line quips and *dichos* made famous by Cantínflas, México's most beloved comic.

My mother took me and my five sisters on a trip to Providencia to visit her mother when I was ten years old. The first film story my mother asked me to recite was "Angelitos Negros," a movie that had impressed her and no one else in nana's household had seen. I remember it was a chilly evening. Family members scurried to retrieve and unroll woven straw *petates* on which they would lay on the floor to settle down for the night. We assembled around a wood-burning fire circle in nana's *Ramada* facing the back yard. My sisters and I huddled together on a *pétate*, along with mamá. We wrapped ourselves with a large blanket to keep warm. Nana's criados, Jaime and Cristina unrolled their *pétates* on the select spot where they would sleep. My nana and intimate family friends who came to visit remained seated. I dutifully recited the sad "Angelitos Negros" story from memory. After I finished the story, my mother and the elders discussed the moral of the story; its implications and the consequences. All agreed: racism was intolerable, as was the inappropriate behavior of the bigoted mother. To be sure, storytelling was an important part of our family culture. I learned to value interesting stories and craved for more. This pursuit inspired me to become an avid reader and to appreciate films, especially classic art cinema.

The recent Friday night of recollections evoked bitter-sweet memories of the influence my mother had on my appreciation for the art of *cuentos* and storytelling. But, it also stirred up the ache of old abandonment issues I have worked to analyze and ultimately suppress. It was during that fateful voyage to México that my mother chose to remain in Providencia, rather than return home to Highgrove with her husband and children. Consequently, I lost contact with Mamá for eleven years until, as a young adult, I traveled to Providencia in search of my mother.

The power of the literary, visual, and performance arts is boundless. Its skilled expression can move and inspire people. Compelling storytelling can influence one's perspective. It has the fantastic power to transport us to another time, another place. Across world cultures, music, theater, cinema, and caricatures have effected social change among people unable to read the written word. México's famous graphic artist José Guadalupe Posada, for example, roused the masses of illiterate peasants to advocate agrarian reform and democracy. He used clever graphics, humorous caricatures, and etchings to illustrate the abuses of the repressive Porfírio Díaz regime. Posada's innovative works incited support of the Mexican Revolution that began in 1910. His illustrations are legendary, widely imitated and reproduced internationally to this day. The arts can be exquisitely educational and transformational. In retrospect, the "Angelitos Negros" cathartic story served as a catalyst in developing my sensitivity, understanding, and appreciation of cultural and racial differences as a positive point of view.

During a business trip to México City in the mid-1980s, I searched for this vintage black and white film. From *la Zona Rosa*, I boarded the Metro to a shopping district to look for "Angelitos Negros" at various music/video stores, markets, and bookstores. It was akin to a treasure-hunting expedition. Not one shop sold it! Disappointed, I began to feel discouraged. *How could this be!* I thought. *This is México City, one of the most cosmopolitan cities in the Americas. It has to be somewhere.* Finally, a shopkeeper suggested that a certain video rental store across from *el Palacio Nacional de Bellas Artes* might have it. Encouraged, I took a taxi to the theater area where I eventually found the store. I proceeded to the counter to request it. The clerk without delay went directly to the drama section and pulled out the only copy they had available. Thrilled, I bought the VHS video tape on the spot. Later, back home in Riverside, I viewed the film again for the first time in over thirty years. The video cover accurately states (in Spanish) that this film is from the gold collection - jewels from the national theater.

What a treasure to be discovered in "Angelitos Negros."

Frances J. Vasquez

Divine Star

For Marion Mitchell-Wilson

In the infinite, benevolent obsidian sky
on an ominous August night
an upward glance into the vast universe
providence gave witness to a bright Star
       soar through the glorious cosmos.

Gracious Marion, generosity of spirit
sublime love of family, friends, community
valiant steward of the precious landscape
uplifting celebrant of poetry, prose
       all literary works Inlandia.

Brilliant, effervescent Superstar
on a mystical, ethereal quest
her earth mission on due course
gallant life intentions, dreams fulfilled
       is sweetly liberated, set free.

Luminous eternal Star
now glorious and Heaven bound
her celestial ascent blessed
advanced, evolved she glided home
       God Bless Marion, a wish come true.

Gran Maestro

Magdaleno (Leno) F. Díaz

> *To laugh often and much; to win the respect of intelligent*
> *people and the affection of children; to earn the appreciation*
> *of honest critics and endure the betrayal of false friends;*
> *to appreciate beauty; to find the best in others; to leave the*
> *world a bit better....*
>
> ~ Ralph Waldo Emerson

The news of your passing saddens me and I mourn you, dear Leno. Beside the sorrow is a sense of gratitude for the auspicious timing to have enjoyed your company only six days before. God blessed you with ninety-five fruitful *primaveras* to grace humanity. I heartily welcomed your invitation to view the *Great Masters of Iberoamerican Folk Art* at the Los Angeles Museum of Natural History. Thank you for sharing what would become our ultimate excursion together.

Our lovely, cheerful visit in your home before we ventured to the museum was magical. We discussed familia, art, books. We chatted joyfully around the dining table enjoying *café con pan dulce* and fresh-picked tangerines from my garden. I took an old 1998 copy of *Phineas Literary Magazine* from Valley College. I wanted to share with you and everyone that it featured two of your *Tata Leno* charcoal drawings: "The Monk" and a head-shot portrait of a woman holding a cigarette in her hand. It felt terrific to see how much you enjoyed seeing the book. "The Monk," you said with a broad smile, "is one of my favorites. How can I get a copy of this *Phineas?*" you inquired. *It was as if you had seen it for the first time*, I thought.

Appreciating the discussion, your admiring wife Elisa, glanced lovingly at you from across the table. With

191

twinkling eyes, she exclaimed lucidly, "He's so handsome!" Afterwards, as we prepared to leave for our museum tour, I quietly approached you and repeated what Elisa had just said. Your face lit up brightly and you smiled. Humbly, you nodded to acknowledge that you had heard the compliment. Yes, your bride of over 65 years still swoons at the sight of her tall, handsome, talented husband.

Your death prompted me to reflect on our four decades-long friendship. My respect and love for you flourished over the years. As I had told you many times, "If I could have chosen my parents, I would have chosen you and Elisa." I'm glad that I publicly declared my esteem for you both during your 65th wedding anniversary *fiesta* last October.

Maestro, you are one of the most remarkable persons in my life and I will forever remember you. I admire who and what you are: authentic, kind, ethical, intelligent, loyal, witty ~ a quintessential renaissance man. A gifted educator, you developed a unique specialty in bilingual curricula development and English-as-a-Second language. While serving as a Master Teacher, you produced model enhanced teaching methods and developed outstanding teacher workshops utilizing puppetry, art, and multi-media techniques.

Among other philanthropic endeavors, you volunteered as a scoutmaster, public library trustee, and founding member of several organizations. As a passionate advocate for civil rights and the Latino community in San Bernardino, you worked with César Chavez, Fred Ross, Cruz Nevarez, and the Community Service Organization. You also served as a Deputy Registrar and registered many new voters. Your love of arts and culture, both as a creator and a consumer is a major part of your legacy.

In jubilant retirement, you, *Tata Leno* cultivated your personal artist brand in the Latino folk art specialty of *nichos* (three-dimensional images of saints) and *rétablos* (altars featuring religious figures) with which you frequently incorporated found objects. Wherever you lived, you curated art exhibitions, thus advancing beauty. We traveled near and far to support *Tata Leno* art exhibitions: San Bernardino, San Antonio, Los Angeles. We swelled with pride to learn you were invited to curate an exhibition of rétablos by the *Instituto Cultural de México* in San Antonio. It was an honor to attend your one-man show of *Tata Leno Nichos* at the *Universidad Nacional Autónoma de México* in San Antonio. Later, when you and Elisa moved to the St. John of God retirement home in Los Angeles, you, gran Maestro gave art lessons to the residents and curated an inaugural exhibition of their art works.

Your company generated wonderful memories: stimulating conversations; excursions and events: plays, concerts, lectures, operas, classic cinema, art galleries, and museums. I'll miss your inimitable, sometimes self-effacing humor. You took pride in having memorized over a hundred jokes both in Spanish and English. It was endearing that you liked to conclude our phone calls with a *chíste*, "You want to hear a joke," you would say. I laughed every time, especially at your hilarious *Cantínflas chístes*, particularly "Cásimiro Guerra" and "El Burro Pendejo."

Maestro, I cherish "La Niña Sentada," your oil-on-canvas painting after Diego Rivera that I acquired as the highest bidder at the *Despedida* event we held in tribute to you and Elisa when you both left San Bernardino to resettle in San Antonio. As you wished, we established a student scholarship fund at Valley College in your and Elisa's honor with the auction proceeds.

I adore my collection of *Tata Leno nichos*: "Nuestra Senora de Guadalupe," "San Francisco," "San Antonio," and the "Red Rock Sacred Heart" the last one that I purchased at your wedding anniversary celebration. These are displayed prominently in my home and their images engraved in my heart. A votive candle glows at the base of a *Tata Leno Nicho* in homage to my best Maestro.

It was a Godsend that the *Grandes Maestros* exhibition would be our grand finale together, as folk art is the genre in which you excelled and gained fame. The *cherry-on-top* to our sweet museum excursion was that your beloved wife accompanied us - just like old times. I was thrilled to see you both enjoy the over eight hundred works by artists from twenty-two Latin American countries. Elisa's gait is still swift, but her slim legs move slightly more rigidly now. With a happy, ever-smiling face, she quietly studied each exhibit carefully reading the captions. And you, in the museum's wheel chair, pondered the exhibits and marveled at the intricate brush strokes of the painted objects. "Oh, look at how beautiful and detailed the carvings of these sculptures" you exclaimed. Dear Leno, you were in harmony with the other Maestros.

On the car ride back home, you expressed a few final wishes regarding your proposed inheritance to your two adult children. Then, I was surprised to hear you say matter-of-factly, "I'm tired. I'm ready to go. *Ya estoy listo pa irme al otro barrio.*" Indeed, you enjoyed a wonderful and distinguished life. You loved deeply, worked diligently, and lived admirably. You laughed often; appreciated and created beauty. It is our good fortune that you left this world substantially better with your humanitarian projects and legacy of social justice and civil rights ~ and a tangible, enduring body of beautiful *Tata Leno Creations*.

It stirred my heart to see you enjoy the *Phineas* book. Right before leaving your home, I offered the book to you so you could read it at your leisure. I said to you, "Keep it, Leno. I'll get it back on our next visit." We embraced with a warmhearted *abrazo*, as we expressed our mutual gratitude and farewell. How could I have known that this would be our last visit? Our last excursion... *nuestro último abrazo.* Those final moments are etched in my thoughts. With your loss, a distinctive epoch of my life has ended. I will miss you and your stories - *chístes.* I value the exquisite memories and delight in my *Tata Leno* art collection. Rest in peace, grand Master. *En paz descanse, gran* Maestro.

Fin

Monalinda Verlengia

I Love Me

28.5 years service
with a rocky start at first;
new beginnings
I knew would be a challenge.
I learned from masters
and promise to do better.
The end is near;
a new door opens
and I walk through
less expectations or fears.
I am the best
for this job.
I wish to share my life
with one who listens
unbeknownst of the result
caring to savor the freshness
of sashimi and sake
spaghetti e pane.

As I walk up a hill
I admire the horizons
still with the desert scene
yet alive with passion
to teach one more lesson:
"Hello, I am your instructor."

Monalinda Verlengia

You are my Angel: strong, intelligent and m-mm Sexy.

From the minute one of us leaves the driveway
I want to run after you as fast as I can and tell you,
"You are wonderful," over and over.
You amaze me, and I am in awe we met.
I cannot tell you enough or show you.
Thank you for making me feel perfect.
With you near me, I feel safe, sexy, smart and loved.
I love everything about you from head to toe.

You plan the moments to perfection.
Every second is an adventure.
The fantasy I had yesterday,
(one you don't even know), you fulfill.
You help me with decisions
even though you let me decide.
I need you so much.
I can't wait to see you.
Although at times I am quiet, even speechless,
my heart, soul and mind is
smokin' for you. I am on fire for you.
I don't know what to say or do first.
Then, when I see you, I cannot keep my hands off you.
I cannot touch you enough.
Life ends far too soon.
Since only One knows our future
and the most perfect plan may change
I say what I feel so you do not forget
Or in case time, as we conceptualize it, expires.
You are perfect and you are wonderful.
I pray God keep you safe on your journey.

Monalinda Verlengia

A Bad Decision: Spouse #2

I had been married for thirteen years, and I had a newborn son, 3 months, a four year old son and a six year old daughter. My first husband had cheated on me fourteen times that I knew of. That came to a halt when I ordered my birth certificates for my three kids (after he had a vasectomy I insisted on). I received three birth certificates, but one was for a different son, not one living with us. I did not need further evidence that once a cheat, always a cheat. I looked at my three month old son, and I knew I would not be living with the father to raise him. It was time for a big change.

Towards the end of my first marriage after I had confronted him about his affairs which he admitted to and suggested an open marriage, I had an affair. It was wonderful and relieving in many ways. I flew to the erotic exotic Halloween festival in San Francisco. I was far enough away to have a great time. When I came home, I couldn't tell anyone about it because it was an affair. I hated that it was a secret.

I asked my first husband to move out after the Christmas holidays before my birthday in late January so as not to rock the boat at home for the children through the holidays. He didn't care about us and the holidays. He went to see his girlfriend and disappeared the entire day on Christmas as he had been doing for years as he lived dual lives. I knew because I had checked his odometer that day and checked the phone bill. The number he frequently called in a neighboring area code and the mileage were coincidentally the same. I looked under the mat on the passenger's side of the car and found photos of a woman and a newborn son who looked remarkably like my husband. I had found the baby momma to the birth certificate

I possessed.

I filed for divorce on my birthday, January 29. I owned 3 quads and that happened to be the last day one could legally ride in the desert in southern California. Needless to say, my birthday was not fun but I did the right thing. I have no regrets.

I placed an ad in the paper for a playmate to go bicycle riding and to go dancing, and be friends. I worded that incorrectly and received twenty five responses in less than twenty-four hours, but I weeded through the replies. I dated a few and selected one; he proposed to me. He fit the bill. Little did I know, he bought a bike to please me and hated bicycling. He bought an Arthur Murray dancing package for us to please me. He hated dancing. I wanted to marry in June but he rushed me and said February would be better. I have regretted rushing from the day he suggested it. That summer while in the pool, my daughter clung to him because she wanted a dad. He overstepped his boundaries throughout the seven years he and I were married.

At dinner one night in January, once again, none of us seemed happy. I asked my daughter what was wrong. She seemed extremely moody and silent. She said something like this: I have a real dad who beats me, a step-dad who molests me and a mom who yells at me. I dropped the glass dish as I was walking to the table to serve dinner. It shattered in a million pieces as the rest of my life came unraveled; I was in horror. She wouldn't speak to me that night, but I knew I had to move forwards and carefully. I had three children and I felt I had jeopardized all our lives, our homes, and everything.

I survived almost 7 years in the second marriage. The only good part I recall was the first year, possibly. He had two older boys and everyone seemed to get along. We travelled often to Baja and the river camping with everyone and everything including their friends in tow. He had completed a small room addition to accommodate our growing family.

That night, when husband (#2) came home and I was cleaning the kitchen, I told him that if he ever did anything to any one of my children, he would go to jail and it would be over. He said that if I ever said anything like that again accusing him, he would kill me. He had to have one up on me always, but this was not something we were going to keep score on. I knew he was dangerous and I had to carefully plan our next move. I dropped the conversation and told each one of my children a huge change would be taking place very soon.

I went to the police department with my three children and we began the process. We filed for a temporary restraining order good for three days since he had threatened to kill me. The police came and escorted him out of the house.

While that went through I filed for a permanent restraining order (which is three years) for all of us and I filed my divorce. We set up a day for my x to gather his belongings which I stacked neatly in boxes by the door. Within a few weeks, the district attorney interviewed my daughter. The interviews were lengthy for each count and brutal for my daughter. She had to relive each moment for each count. The D.A. filed three counts of lewd and vicious child molestation. My daughter said it was too hard for her to retell any more counts. The DA said three counts would be sufficient for a conviction because of the details she revealed and agreed that retelling was hurting my daughter. She would testify against her step-father.

It took years to close this case. His mother offered my daughter $50,000 to keep her son out of jail. We refused. The father, husband #1, has not paid child support and owes $83,000 to date. The step dad served five years in a state penitentiary. To this day, he has not shown any remorse. I filed a life-long restraining order, and the Judge granted one for fifty years covering my life time. His picture, when googled, comes up as child molester every time. My second marriage was the biggest mistake of my life.

Hopefully, now that over ten years has passed and all my children are over twenty-one, I will someday meet someone wonderful. Life continues, and I cannot forget the tragedy we lived through. He threatened us to the last minute before his sentence that he would pay us back. I have three wonderful supportive children. I was afraid to raise all of them alone, but I did it with the help of true good friends.

There was nowhere to run or hide. A shelter would have been temporary. I have mottos I live by: protect your children. The grass is not greener on the other side. It's only green where you water it, and for us that was right here; finally, and always, do the right thing. Had he killed me, where would my children be today?

The Bumpy Road to Becoming a Writer

Talk to just about anyone and it seems they have a story to tell, a book to write—if only.

If only they had the time.

If only they had the skill.

If only they didn't have to work, raise kids, had a quiet space…

Or if only someone of authority hadn't devastated their spirit and self-confidence.

Like so many others, I have always wanted to write—and had my list of "if onlies." I always thought, well, I'll get around to it—someday.

Someday is upon me. Now that I am in my seventh decade, I realize there isn't much time left. If I don't write now, I never will.

In 1968, I was a shy, idealistic young mother when I bravely signed up for an evening creative writing class at Riverside City College (RCC). In those days, RCC made returning to school a fairly simple thing to do. At the time, no one had ever encouraged me to go beyond high school; it had not even seemed to be a possibility. Nonetheless, I longed for "an education."

I thought it would be a good idea to start with something I thought I could master—writing. The teacher, Mr. Bowers, seemed to like what I wrote. It was so exciting! I could hardly wait for each week's class as I eagerly completed my assignments. I was high on the joy of it all. I had graduated from "old" Poly High School nine years earlier when Terracina Drive still intersected the two campuses and Miss May Henry was my English teacher. What made going to college even better was how I loved the beautiful RCC campus and its old buildings, especially those in the Quad. I felt like Emily Dickinson at Amherst Academy.

After the seeming success in Mr. Bowers' class, I was emboldened enough to sign up for Creative Writing II, even though my then-husband was not enthusiastic about it. I couldn't understand; I always expressed my pride in him for his accomplishments. When he later had an affair, the "other woman" told me he said that I liked to read and used big words a lot. I had not realized this was a fault worthy of justifying an affair which led to the end of our ten-year marriage. I had never flaunted vocabulary or even thought about it—I only knew I loved to read—and hoped I could write.

Back then, houses still lined Terracina Drive; I would walk past them on my way to my evening class. It was also a time when Cheri Jo Bates was murdered and left dead among those houses sometime around Halloween. Her murder was never solved.

I was not deterred.

No, my disapproving husband could not deter me from my educational quest. My first experience had left me joyful and, perhaps for the first time, confident that I could write. Nor could a recent unsolved murder so close to campus deter me. But something else more powerful could not only deter me, it shattered my determination and self confidence.

The next instructor, Mr. M, was very different than Mr. Bowers. He scared the wits out of me and, on more than one occasion, put me down. Once, I wrote something that he might have actually liked, something that seemed to meet the symbolic criteria he was seeking. The assignment was to re-write a scene from an Ernest Hemingway novel. Instead of saying anything positive, he asked "Did you mean to do this?"

Of course I did!

Another time, he began to read some of the previous

week's assignments. "Some of these are really quite dreadful," he said in a most dreadful tone—and began reading mine. His voice could be rich and powerful—or not, depending on how he chose to read. He could have read a recipe and made you *believe*! Preheat the oven! Melt the butter! Beat the eggs! Fold in the flour! Hallelujah! Amen, praise the lord and bake the cake!

The words I had so painstakingly crafted turned to shit as his voice was now a dead, expressionless monotone. I burned with shame.

But the worst time of all was when he looked right at me and said "What is God?"

He scared me so badly, I swear, I couldn't have told you my name at that moment. It was as if a blinding white-hot sheet enveloped my brain into blank nothingness.

"Um…an all powerful being who looks after us…" I began, my voice quaking.

Bang!

His fist pounded the desk. "That's Johnson you're talking about!" he thundered, referring to President Lyndon Johnson. The answer he was seeking was "God Is Love".

Humiliated, I wanted the floor in that beloved old building in my beautiful Amherst Quad to mercifully open up and swallow me, right then and there.

It took me another ten years to be brave enough to take another class—longer than that to think I could write anything worthwhile. In the course of my continuing education at RCC, I had two English teachers whom I greatly respected disagree with Mr. M's dreadful opinion of me.

Tom Johnson, known on campus as a demanding but fair instructor, gave me one of only two A's in his English class that semester. He wrote that my paper on Emily Dickinson "made all the right moves." It earned a very meaningful A.

Another English professor, Charles Walker, a short, stooped, gray-haired man, told me that I *must* write, that I was good. Really good. And yet, their words, their grades, their praise, could not erase what Mr. M. had burned into my psyche.

In spite of Mr. M, I nonetheless went on to write several well-received op-ed columns for *The Press-Enterprise*, our local newspaper. I wrote a column for my home town newspaper in North Dakota for more than seven years—even though I had left there in 1957. One friend, an English teacher, called me Emily Dickinson reincarnated. Another compared my writing to that of Harper Lee.

Yet, Mr. M's words still rang in my ears. Years later, I had the opportunity to tell him he had nipped my creativity in the bud. "It must have been during one of my cruel periods," he said, arrogantly, unapologetically.

In my entire twenty-year-plus quest to get the "education" I so desired, the C from Mr. M was the only one I ever received.

There is a famous quote by historian and author Henry Adams that says: "A teacher affects eternity; he can never tell where his influence stops."

The quote is often used to suggest the positive influence a teacher might have; however, it is equally important to remember that a teacher's influence can be negative as well. Cruel instructors too, can "affect eternity" by destroying a student's spirit and desire to learn. What might they have become if they weren't stopped in their tracks? Fortunately, I had teachers like Tom Johnson and Charles Walker and others—as well as encouraging friends. Thanks to them, I was ultimately able to achieve the "education" that was so important to me.

And now, as I contemplate my own mortality at the mid-point of my seventh decade, will I put all of the "if-onlies" and deterrences aside and get down to the writing I always meant to do?

    We shall see.

(This essay was written as a result of a prompt by Jo Scott-Coe on why I write.)

The Empirical Road to Becoming an Accidental Teacher

I never intended to be a teacher. It was an accident.

It had taken me 20 years to get the education I so desperately wanted. I took my first college course at Riverside City College (RCC) in 1968; I graduated from Cal State San Bernardino (CSUSB) in 1988, the same year my third child graduated from high school.

All during my educational quest, I joked that I was 35, 39, 43, whatever, and still didn't know what I "wanted to be when I grew up." I only knew that I wanted something more, something called an education—a *college* education; however, since I didn't know what I "wanted to be," it was difficult to zero in on a major.

The path was difficult. I experienced roadblocks and setbacks—a broken marriage or two, single motherhood, food stamps, health issues, a cruel instructor, low-paying jobs and more—but, like the tortoise in the fable of the tortoise and the hare, I plugged along until I reached a finish line. I earned a Bachelor's Degree in Human Development. It encompassed the subjects I was most interested in—Sociology, Psychology and Anthropology.

I was now married to someone who had a lot of free time; he liked to go to movies and baseball games while I hoped to finally get serious about writing. I took the CBEST (California Basic Skills Education Test) which was a requirement to be a substitute teacher in the state of California. This would give me the flexibility to write and be able to spend time going to movies, baseball games and having Friday date days. I was nearly 50 years old at the time.

The Riverside County Office of Education (RCOE)

provided a program called Esperanza, an educational opportunity for teen mothers. It enabled them to go to high school during pregnancy and after the birth of their child, thanks to on-site child care. Esperanza classes were designed to educate teens about pregnancy and how to care for their child after birth. Classrooms were scattered throughout Riverside County, usually located on the site of a high school campus. After I was hired, I soon found myself frequently requested, including a high school in the Jurupa area. There, the teacher was on maternity leave; one day, the students locked the unpopular long-term sub in the bathroom adjacent to the class. After that, she did not return and I was asked to take the long-term position. The principal of the program told me I was a natural and wouldn't I consider becoming a *real* teacher? I didn't want to. I wanted to have more control over my time, my life. But, I took the long-term assignment.

I swear, I flew by the seat of my pants those first few weeks. After all, I hadn't taken any classes on how to be a teacher. Long-term was different than showing up to sub for a day or two. Fortunately, my years of motherhood and a lifetime of experiences kicked in. At first, I tried to follow how I thought I was "supposed" to teach as well as accept the awkward, impersonal arrangement of the classroom. Everything felt stiff, unnatural.

At the same time, I was reading *Long Quiet Highway* by Natalie Goldberg. In it, she wrote of trying to force herself to be the teacher she had been trained to be; she was teaching at a school for Native American children in New Mexico and their behavior was atrocious. She was miserable and realized teaching was not her true calling after all. Being a writer was.

She went to the principal and gave her notice. For the next two weeks, she let loose and followed her natural instincts— when it rained, she took the kids outdoors, challenging them to see if they could run between the raindrops. She plucked a piece of sage, inhaled deeply and invited them to try it. Suddenly, they were cooperative. They were wonderful. They were ready to learn.

It was as if Natalie Goldberg gave me permission to be the teacher I was meant to be whether I knew it or not. It was as if Destiny Herself had grabbed me by the hand and said, "You *will* be a teacher!" It was a calling.

I began doing things in a way that felt natural to me. Soon, we were putting together an article for the school newspaper on how pregnant students were often judged by others. The students were incredible. When the state PTA president and her entourage wanted to visit an Esperanza classroom, the principal brought her to mine—a *substitute* teacher's! A sub that did not yet have her full credential—but those girls made me look great. Although many years have passed, I still feel love for them in my heart.

After the regular teacher returned, the principal asked if I would be willing to do home teaching—going to the homes of students who would have difficulty even in an Esperanza classroom. It was a time before a GPS system could help us find where we were going; I was provided a county car to drive and addresses of the students I was to teach. Somehow, I managed to find my way to out-of-the way places in that lumbering old white county station wagon.

One pregnant student was 12; she could barely read at a first-grade level. I designed homework I thought she could handle—such as providing simple books, telling her she must read to her baby when it came. One time her mother left her homework at the methadone clinic. Another was living in a house with no electricity; in the semi-darkness, I had to step around the dog poop on the floor. Another had an 11-month-old and was expecting twins. She was going to give them up for adoption but had them prematurely; she fell in love with them and could not give them up. She was ill-prepared for three babies under the age of one. She needed a crib. I delivered the one I had purchased for a grandchild who had outgrown it; I was so happy that day, I wanted to sing all the way to Elsinore and back.

From there I went to a self-contained Esperanza classroom housed at a continuation school in Moreno Valley. When the continuation school needed a full-time English teacher, they hired me.

Although I still had hoops to jump through in order to obtain my full credential—including passing the SSAT test—I became a for-real teacher at the age of 50. This gave me the opportunity to be the kind of teacher I wish I could have had. I would not be like Felix Gunther, my junior high teacher in North Dakota who humiliated me in front of the class. I would not be like Mr. M., a cruel college professor.

It was amazing how my English students bloomed when provided with positive encouragement. My heart soared when one of them would say, "I didn't know I could do that" when he discovered the magic in his writing. There were times I simply talked to them. The words tumbled out of my mouth as if they were guided by some unknown force. When I spoke of my own despair and desire to commit suicide many years prior, Gwen told me it had prevented her own. Each week we had a Friday Freewrite; it was amazing—and scary—to read some of the things they were willing to share with me. James wrote of his suicide attempt; I was so grateful to see him alive and well in my classroom the following Monday. In another freewrite, he wrote about how his mother had tried to kill him.

I wanted them to expand their vocabularies and learn words like aficionado. To help them remember how to pronounce it, I drew a fish in an auto. Or, I walked around the room blowing bubbles and asked them to write everything they could about bubbles. I put positive, thought-provoking sayings on the board that seemed to resonate with them.

I kept water and crackers in my room. How can a student concentrate if they are hungry or homeless or just fought their father for a gun? How could they concentrate on passing the myriad of mandated tests if they were fighting to pass the biggest test of all? The one called survival. Of course, not all of my students came from difficult home situations or had spent time in Juvenile Hall or attempted suicide. They might have been lazy and got behind on credits. They may have ditched school too often. They might have been turned off to writing or reading or learning itself by a too-harsh teacher. It didn't matter how they got there—once they ended up in my classroom, it was my opportunity and privilege to try to awaken their desire to get an "education."

If I mentioned that I taught at a continuation school, people would say I was brave or that they felt sorry for me, working with all those "bad" kids. No, this was my niche, my joy. I belonged there. When I retired at the age of 65, my spirit wanted to continue but, unfortunately, my body said no. I will always be grateful that I ended my working days doing something I was so passionate about, that I had the opportunity to make a difference in the lives of my students—even though teaching had never been my plan.

And, once again, there is that famous quote by Henry Adams that says: "A teacher affects eternity; he can never tell where his influence stops."

I hope that my students remember me—and that my influence continues to ripple through their lives in a positive way. I just wonder how many of them realize that they, too, influenced me.

(This essay was a result of a prompt by Jo Scott-Coe's prompt to bring a book to our workshop that we considered a personal "sacred text." Mine was Long Quiet Highway by Natalie Goldberg.)

Jean Waggoner

Gracious Marion

We never know how high we are
'Till we are called to rise,
And then, if we are true to plan,
Our statures touch the skies.

—*Emily Dickinson* (from "Aspiration")

This is the night of the end of summer,
your bright moon rising over Citrus Park,
full, golden and ripe with our grief
as we drift from the Tudor-beamed hall
to the garden of your earthly delights.

This is the night of our fondest memories,
old photos, songs, prayers and dreams,
with your joyous laughter just out of hearing,
amid an ambience of fine linens, flowers,
filled glasses and unforgettable hospitality.

This is the night of our standing without you,
that high bar internal, now, your blessings
given through gracious validation
of our talents, offerings, aspirations
and ability to carry on in your afterglow.

Biographies

Celena Diana Bumpus, BA, AODA is CEO, Editor and Book Designer of three publishing houses. For the last three years, she has taught four ongoing creative writing workshops at the Janet Goeske Senior Center in Riverside, CA. Two classes are dedicated to the writings of USA Veterans and their families. She is the published author of the poetry collection, Confessions (1998, The Inevitable Press). Her personal essay was published in the textbook, Street Lit: Representing the Urban Landscape (2014, Scarecrow Press). Her prose and poetry have appeared in the following publications: 2012 Writing From Inlandia (2012, Heyday Books), Verse/Chorus: A Call and Response Anthology (2013, Scarecrow Press), 2013 Writing From Inlandia (2013, Heyday Books), Invisible Memoirs (2014, Memoir Journal), Orangelandia: The Literature of Inlandia Citrus (2014, Inlandia Institute), On the Rusk Literary Journal (2014) and online at Pen 2 Paper (2014). Her website is www.islandsforwriters.blogspot.com. Please visit her profile for her social media links

Dr. Deenaz P. Coachbuilder is an educator, artist, poet and environmental advocate. She is a retired school principal and professor in special education, and a consulting speech pathologist. Deenaz is a Fulbright scholar, and the recipient of numerous awards, most recently, President Barak Obama's "Volunteer Service"award. Deenaz's poetry, commentaries and essays have appeared in national and regional publications and poetry blogs in the U.S. and India. Her recent book of poems, "Imperfect Fragments," has been received with critical acclaim both here and abroad. Deenaz has exhibited her paintings in oil in diverse venues, including a solo show. Deenaz resides in Riverside, Seattle and Mumbai, India. She enjoys reading, travelling, gardening, going for long walks, family and close friends, staying involved in the Indian American community and the Zoroastrian Association of California. She particularly cherishes being a wife and mother, and a recent grandmother.

Carlos E. Cortés is professor emeritus of history at the University of California, Riverside. His most recent book is his autobiography, *Rose Hill: An Intermarriage before Its Time* (Berkeley, CA: Heyday, 2012). Other books include *The Children Are Watching: How the Media Teach about Diversity and The Making—and Remaking—of a Multiculturalist,* published by Teachers College Press. Cortés is general editor of *Multicultural America: A Multimedia Encyclopedia* (Sage, 2013), scholar-in-residence with Univision Communications, and Creative/Cultural Advisor for Nickelodeon's Peabody-award-winning children's television series, "Dora the Explorer," and its sequel, "Go, Diego, Go!," for which he received the 2009 NAACP Image Award. He also travels the country performing his one-person autobiographical play, *A Conversation with Alana: One Boy's Multicultural Rite of Passage,* while he co-wrote the book and lyrics for the musical, *We Are Not Alone: Tomás Rivera—A Musical Narrative,* which premiered in 2011.

Laurel V. Cortés: At 17, I went to Mexico City alone to attend the University of Mexico. The experience changed my life and, after majoring in Spanish and minoring in Comparative Literature at San Diego State University, I worked for 28 years at the University of California, Riverside, in – guess what? – the Department of Literatures and Languages. The job perfectly suited my interests, and it's fun now to do a bit of writing on my own.

Since she was nine years old, **Sylvia Clarke** (MA, TESOL) has enjoyed writing. Some of what she has written has appeared in print, but knowing there was more to learn, she joined her husband, Wil, in not only taking a class but also participating in Matthew Nadelson's workshop. These experiences have rekindled the fires as has the opportunity to see something of hers in print. Thanks, Inlandia!

Wil Clarke recently retired from roughly forty years of teaching mathematics at the university level. Born and educated through his sophomore year in college in South Africa, he finished his undergraduate education and met Sylvia, his wife of fifty years, at Andrews University in Michigan. After doing graduate work at the University of Iowa, he taught for five years at Ikizu Secondary School in Tanzania and four years in South Africa. He has published a number of articles on mathematics, computer science, and history in several journals. He also authored two mathematics distance learning courses for Griggs University. He attends a writing class at the Janet Goeske Senior Center taught by Celena Bumpus and an Inlandia writing workshop with Matt Nadelson. He is president of the Riverside Stamp Club. He loves driving across country and four-wheeling in the desert and enjoys body surfing and bouldering.

Don Dietz is a retired high school teacher with a Master Degree in Industrial Education and Counseling. Not only has he become a Stained Glass Artist in retirement, but during summer visits to Idyllwild he has gotten inspired to do some writing and he is learning to paint while basking in the glories of Idyllwild.

Ellen Estilai received her B.A. in Art from the University of California, Davis, and her M. A. in English Language and Literature from the University of Tehran. A former executive director of the Riverside Arts Council and the Arts Council for San Bernardino County, she taught literature and writing at the University of Tehran, Cal State Bakersfield and the University of San Francisco's external degree program. Her essay, "Front Yard Fruit," originally published in *Alimentum: The Literature of Food*, is included in *New California Writing 2011* (Heyday) and was selected as a Notable Essay in *The Best American Essays 2011*. Her work has also appeared in the journals *Phantom Seed* and *Broad!*, the anthologies *Slouching Towards Mount Rubidoux Manor* (Summer 2010) and *(In) Visible Memoirs, Vol. 2*. (2013), the Riverside *Press-Enterprise*, and the *Inlandia Literary Journeys* blog. Ellen is a founding member of the Inlandia Institute Board of Directors.

Nan Friedley is a retired special education teacher originally from Indiana. She has participated in the Riverside Inlandia workshop for the past two years along with other local writing groups. Her poetry has been published in the 2013 Inlandia anthology and "Three" by PushPen Press. Thanks to fellow workshop members and leaders for the encouragement you've given me to keep writing.

Françoise Frigola, a regular attendee of the Idyllwild Inlandia workshop, was born and raised in France. She writes spontaneously, often on current social issues. With an MA in transpersonal psychology she sees the astrological chart as a map of the person's psyche. For several years, she wrote a column on *Counseling Astrology* in Aspect magazine. She has a BS in Computer science and business administration and over 45 years of experience as a computer consultant. She is also an internationally exhibited and collected artist.

Marie Griffiths has participated in the Ontario workshop led by Charlotte Davidson. Marie Griffiths earned her PhD in English from The University of California, Riverside and currently resides in Fontana. Retired from careers in nursing and teaching, she enjoys creative writing and the camaraderie of fellow writers. Her writing has appeared in Writing from Inlandia Anthology and Fresh Ink, the publication of the Inland Empire branch of the California Writers' Club.

Teresa Halliburton (T Qi) currently works at Idyllwild School for the Arts and national charter school, Summit Academy CA. She volunteers at the library and offers her meditation, exercise and writing programs at shaolinclinics@gmail.com.

Karen Rae Kraut has been blending story, song and creative movement in schools, libraries, museums and theatres from California to East Tennessee since 1990. She has toured for the Smithsonian, and was commissioned by the McCallum Theatre to create a storyteller's version of Mozart's "The Magic Flute." Karen's CD, "Cooler Water Cora and Other Stories," is the winner of an iParenting Media Award for Audio Excellence and a National Parenting Publications Honors Award. She has performed for Riverside's First Sundays program since its inception in 1997. She has a Masters Degree in Storytelling from East Tennessee State University and was recently named a State Liaison for the National Storytelling Network. Find out more about Karen and see video on YouTube and at www.karenraekraut.com.

Michael Orlich began writing poetry in 2011. Since then, he has hosted a small monthly poetry group in his home in Reche Canyon, in Colton. He has lived in the IE since 2008 and works at Loma Linda University as a preventive medicine physician and researcher in nutritional epidemiology. His poem "Communications Tower" was published in 2015 in *Inlandia: A Literary Journey*. He participated in the Ontario workshop.

Jane O'Shields-Hayner is a writer and visual artist. She writes essays, non-fiction, biographical and historical fiction, and poetry; and she produces and shows visual art. In both art forms she addresses universal issues and their relationship to all of life and individual life journeys. Jane has bachelor's degrees in Fine Arts, with a specialty in art; and in education, from Texas Christian University. She also has a Master's degree in Occupational Therapy from Loma Linda University. Jane has a background in teaching art and other subjects and in community and global activism. She practices occupational therapy with a specialty in home health care throughout Riverside County. Jane's husband, Bill Hayner is also an artist, an activist and an educator. They have two young children and two adult daughters and they live in Corona, in the foothills of the Santa Ana Mountains. She and her family are members of the Inland Valley Monthly Meeting of the Religious Society of Friends, also known as Quakers. Jane's work has recently been published in Tiferet Journal, Friends Journal, and The Manifest Station. She has recently shown artwork in The Studio Door Gallery in San Diego and other venues.

Felix Sepulveda was born in 1949, and raised in Redlands, California, in the 1950s. As a child, he was held back in second grade, but his curiosity about learning was peaked when his father bought him a set of Wonder Books. Felix graduated from Redlands High School and attended Crafton Hills College and the University of California Riverside before he was hired as a Probation Officer for San Bernardino County. After 15 years he left the Department and began working with Pre-Paid Legal Services a multi-level marketing company.

He became dismayed after attaining the rank of Executive Director when he found continued monetary success to be running on a treadmill made of time from his life. It was never ending and unenjoyable. He has discovered writing and has been published in the Sand Canyon Review and has won a writing contest at Fanstory.com. Being published in Writing from Inlandia has reignited his love of writing.

Marsha Schuh and her husband Dave are currently remodeling the 88-year old home in Ontario that they moved into as a young couple. She teaches English at CSUSB and is working on a collection of poems—inspired by her early morning walks—about Ontario and its history. Marsha's poetry has appeared in literary journals such as *Pacific Review, Badlands, The Sand Canyon Review, Shuf,* and *Inlandia.*

Suzanne Shimaya appreciates that the Inlandia workshop experience has given her the opportunity to revisit some long-neglected fiction projects. She would especially like to thank Inlandia workshop leader and fiction writer Charlotte Davidson and poet Cathy Henley-Erickson for their gentle advice on story revision and for their encouragement.

David Stone moved to Riverside, CA to attend graduate school at La Sierra University, where he met his future wife Cathy. He has taught English at Loma Linda Academy for more than a decade. David enjoys writing, cooking, and exploring nature in Redlands, CA with his wife and two children.

As a clinical psychologist and spiritual director, **Judith E. Turian,** Ph.D. assists her clients by helping them establish or deepen their spiritual lives. While on active duty in the US Navy, Dr. Turian was the clinical director of the Alcoholic Rehabilitation Service at the Naval Hospital in Long Beach,

CA. where she was influenced by the power of Twelve Step spirituality. Her book *God: A Relationship Guide*, helps people establish and deepen a relationship with God. Based on her personal life and clinical experience, her

Gudelia Vaden is a retired preschool teacher with a BA degree in Liberal Studies with a Bilingual-Bicultural Emphasis. In retirement, she has developed several hobbies: gardening, line dancing, watercolor painting and creative writing. During the last two years, she has enjoyed the Inlandia Creative Writing Workshops where she has been encouraged to write. She resides in Riverside, CA with her husband Tom and black and white Chihuahua named Pepper.

Tom Vaden is a retired statistician with a MS degree in Mathematics. In retirement, he has taken up several new hobbies: gardening, line dancing, and creative writing. During the last two years, he has enjoyed the Inlandia Creative Writing Workshops where he has been encouraged to write. He resides in Riverside, CA with his wife Delia and a black and white very spoiled Chihuahua named Pepper.

Frances J. Vasquez resides in Riverside. She has a diverse background in public service, and was the Executive Director of Other Cultures, Inc., an international student exchange program specializing in exchanges between Mexico, Central America, Canada, and the U.S. She attended Inland schools and graduated with BS and MBA degrees from the University of California, Riverside. An aficionada of arts and letters, Frances enjoys attending and organizing cultural events.

Monalinda Verlengia has been a southern California English community college teacher for over thirty years. She has been writing diaries, stories, essays and poems since she was age six. Her works have been published in newspapers and books both online and in print. She continues to write daily. She is excited to be working with Inlandia! Now that her three children are over age twenty-one, she remarried in 2015. She takes care of her ninety-two year old mother in her home, and runs her mom's hotel, Aloha Hotel Palm Springs, as well. A novel on the forty-five years in Palm Springs as an inn keeper is in the works!

Jean Waggoner established Idyllwild's Inlandia Writing Workshop in the summer of 2010. A "freeway flier" with a Master's from CSU Fullerton, Jean teaches English and ESL at community colleges in Riverside County. Her work includes story-telling, essays, fine arts reviews, advertising copy and poetry that has appeared in on-line and print publications, including business journals, the National Poetry Anthology, Phantom Seed and Inlandia publications. She has read poetry at Inlandia and Idyllwild community events and at the Poetry Week in San Miguel de Allende, Guanajuato, Mx. (Jan. 2009). Jean recently co-authored with Douglas Snow *The Freeway Flier and the Life of the Mind* (ISBN # 978-1-4568-3119-6 paperback, with e-book available at Amazon, soon).

Mae Wagner has lived in the Inlandia area since 1957 and has been a member of the Inlandia workshop since its beginning in 2008. She is a mother of three, grandmother of seven and great-grandmother of four. She writes under her maiden name after having been married a couple of times too many. She lives in Redlands with her husband, Alex Marinello and her dog Sophie.

About the Inlandia Institute

The Inlandia Institute is a regional non-profit literary center. We seek to bring focus to the richness of the literary enterprise that has existed in this region for ages. The mission of the Inlandia Institute is to recognize, support and expand literary activity in all of its forms through community programs in the Inland Empire, thereby deepening people's awareness, understanding, and appreciation of this unique, complex and creatively vibrant region.

The Institute publishes high quality regional writing in print and electronic form including books published in partnership with Heyday under the Inlandia Institute imprint as well as independent Inlandia Institute publications.

Inlandia presents free public literary programming featuring authors who live in, work in, and/or write about Inland Southern California.

We also provide Creative Literacy Programs for children and youth and hold creative writing workshops for teens and adults.

In addition, every two years the Inlandia Institute appoints a distinguished jury panel from outside of the region to name an Inlandia Literary Laureate who serves as an ambassador for the Inlandia Institute, promoting literature, creative literacy, and community throughout the entire Inlandia region. To date, Laureates include Susan Straight (2010-12), Gayle Brandeis (2012-14), and Juan Delgado (2014-16).

To learn more about the Inlandia Institute please visit our website at www.InlandiaInstitute.org.

Other Inlandia Publications

Independent Inlandia Imprint Publications

No Easy Way: Integrating Riverside Schools – A Victory for Community
Arthur L. Littleworth
Edited by Dawn Hassett
Foreword by Dr. V.P. Franklin
Introduction by Susan Straight

Tia's Tamale Trouble
Julianna Cruz, author
Tracie Lents, illustrator

Orangelandia: The Literature of Inland Citrus
Edited by Gayle Brandeis

Dos Chiles/Two Chilies
Julianna Cruz

2011 Writing from Inlandia: Work of the Inlandia Creative Workshops
Edited by the Inlandia Institute Publications Committee

2012 Writing from Inlandia: Work of the Inlandia Creative Workshops
Edited by the Inlandia Institute Publications Committee

2013 Writing from Inlandia: Work of the Inlandia Creative Workshops
Edited by the Inlandia Institute Publications Committee

Heyday Inlandia Imprint Books

Empire
Lewis deSoto (forthcoming)

Vital Signs
Juan Delgado and Thomas McGovern

Rose Hill: An Intermarriage before Its Time
Carlos Cortès

No Place for a Puritan: The Literature of California's Deserts
Edited by Ruth Nolan

Backyard Birds of the Inland Empire
Sheila N. Kee

Dream Street
Douglas F. McCulloh

Inlandia:A Literary Journey Through California's Inland Empire
Edited by Gayle Wattawa with an introduction by Susan Straight

Inlandia Electronic Publications

Inlandia: A Literary Journey, an on-line journal
Edited by Cati Porter

Audio Guide
Inlandia: A Literary Journey Through California's Inland Empire
Moderated by Gayle Brandeis

Inlandia Literary Journeys Blog
http://www.localauthors.pe.com

INLANDIA
INSTITUTE

www.ingramcontent.com/pod-product-compliance
Lightning Source LLC
Chambersburg PA
CBHW070107260626
47160CB00004B/1352